MW01705461

The Blanket of Bones

Gloria "Fire Eyes" Wilson
and
Frank "Standing Storm" Wilson

PublishAmerica
Baltimore

First printing

ISBN: 1-4241-3048-4
PUBLISHED BY PUBLISHAMERICA, LLLP
www.publishamerica.com
Baltimore

Printed in the United States of America

Dedication

This book is dedicated to all who are young and old, who dream and refuse to allow anyone to take their dreams away.

And to our children and our grandchildren, as a reminder that what you believe is what you will achieve, and with God, the Great Good Spirit, all things are possible for you.

Acknowledgment

We, Gloria Fire Eyes and Frank Standing Storm Wilson, would like to give thanks to all who made this book a reality. There are so many people and events that have helped shape us into who we are today. We are the by-products of our parents, their parents and so on. We can choose to stay as we are or to learn from our ancestors in order to grow spiritually. The more we strive to grow spiritually the less we are like our physical ancestors and more like our true spiritual ancestor, Kijii wasi manato (Great Good Spirit) or M'sum8a (Grandfather) or GOD as many call the Creator.

It is this first ancestor we would like to give thanks for the many lessons sent, all not always easy to accept, but always needed.

We would also like to give thanks to our sacred mother, Gia Tula (Earth) for allowing me, Frank, as a boy to go into the woods and receive the many lessons from the trees, the four-legged animals and all the winged ones, along with all the creepy crawlers. These lessons allowed me to see that we are all connected to each of these both physically and spiritually, and when we hurt any of these or our neighbor, we hurt ourselves. My love and thanks to my M'sum8a (Grandfather) Brewer for his teachings. Although he has walked in the spirit realm for a long time, he has still been able to teach me. NYWEH (Thank You)

We would also like to thank our sister, Anita, who also walks in the realm of spirits for her wisdom, words and lessons. Although at times they were received begrudgedly. Her outlook on life was at times quite odd, but always helpful.

I, Frank, would like to thank my sister, Gloria Fire Eyes, who started this book about my visions and escapades in the woods, along with my imagination. As a child you were always there to help me. You held me when I was hurt or scared; you calmed me to sleep when I could not sleep. You taught me to tie my shoes and to button my clothes (not an easy task as I was left-handed).

We would also give thanks to our mother, Ruth Naomi, who in the best way she could, held us together as a family in spite of all the trials and tribulations we faced then.

We especially would like to thank Melissa, Gloria's daughter. Melissa, you made it possible for this book to be completed. (She knows how to work the computer.)

Thanks to the rest of our family and tribe. We love you each one and pray that we can walk this path together, both spiritually and physically for a long time to come.

We want to thank the publisher (PublishAmerica) who, for whatever reason, saw a possibility in these writings and chose to publish them. NYWEH (Thank you)

Kijimanatoaudeinuhuk peh Tanakia
Gloria FireEyes and Frank Standing Storm Wilson

Chapter 1

It was early summer and a very special day for the Thomas family. Little did they know they were beginning an adventure they would never forget.

Sarah could not sleep the night before because she was so excited about moving to their new house. Sarah, who was six years old, adored her older brother Franky. His sense of adventure and excitement always made their days together fun. And, although this move to a new home had enticed Franky's love for exploring, he was still saddened about leaving his friends behind.

As the sun rose this morning, Franky lay in his bed listening to the sounds of his mother running about. His father's voice echoed as he talked with the movers about what furniture to take and what to leave. The sorting and packing had gone on for weeks, but now the day had finally arrived.

Franky was a curious boy, always tinkering with things just to see how they worked. This morning, he was thinking of the new places he might explore and the new things he would find in his house. His mother had told him that the house they bought was almost a hundred years old. Franky thought back to their conversation at dinner a couple of nights ago.

"Franky, did you know that the land our new house sits on used to be part of an Indian village?"

"Really, Mom? You mean with wigwams, horses and hunting parties?" Franky excitedly asked.

"Yes," answered his mother, "why you might even be able of find some arrowheads or something buried in the backyard!"

"Hmm," thought Franky, "maybe, some of the neighbors could tell me more about the Indians who used to live there."

Franky often daydreamed about the days long ago, when villages of Indians were all over the land. Just the day before, his last day of school, he found it even more difficult to pay attention and concentrate.

Franky imagined how the village was probably surrounded by trees with maybe a river flowing below. In his mind's eye, he could see the children playing hunting games and splashing about in the river. Also, during this time, his mind drifted to thinking about the move and the new house. As he began to feel a little more excited, he realized that there just might be an adventure after all. There were fields and old barns to explore and hide in. All with a true life history of Indians! Surely, there would be many new things to learn and experience.

"Franky? Franky! Can you answer the question?" his teacher had asked.

"Uh, ma'am? Were you talking to me?" Franky asked shyly. The class burst into laughter. The teacher only shook her head because she knew that once again Franky had been daydreaming.

Later that night, Franky resumed his dream as he snuggled down in his bed. His native adventures seemed to just get going in his dream world, when suddenly his bedroom door burst open.

Sarah came running in shouting excitedly, "Franky! Get up, get up we're moving today!" Sarah ran across the room and jumped on Franky's bed. He grabbed her playfully and began to tickle her. Morning had indeed arrived.

"Franky! Sarah! Breakfast! Hurry up now, we've got a lot to do today," mother called.

"Okay," they both said at once.

Sarah went downstairs, and Franky changed out of his pajamas and followed.

As he sat down at the table, his father said to him, "Son, I know you really don't want to move, but you will make new friends. And, we will be back, every once in a while, to visit." Franky nodded and smiled at his father.

At first he didn't want to move at all, but now, the more he daydreamed, he was not feeling quite so bad about it. Actually, the closer the time came to leave, the more excited he became.

Finally, the movers were gone and everything was finished.

Just as the Thomas family was pulling out of the driveway, Sarah shouted, "Wait! I HAVE TO GO TO THE BATHROOM!" Franky just rolled his eyes. His father pulled back into the drive and Sarah and her mother went back into the house.

Once again, Franky's father resumed his speech about all the good things there was about moving, in hopes of picking up his spirits. Franky listened quietly without comment. Sarah and her mother returned and finally they began the long drive to their new home.

They had been driving for quite a long time, when Sarah, in her usually irritating way, announced "I HAVE TO GO TO THE BATHROOM AGAIN."

"Can't you hold it for a while?" Franky impatiently asked Sarah. "We'll never get there at this rate!"

"Don't be so impatient with your sister Franky," said his father, "We'll get there. Keep a look out for somewhere to pull over."

Franky mumbled an apology to Sarah then turned to watch out the window. After a few minutes of watching the endless countryside, Franky spotted a run down old gas station coming up on the right side.

"There's one, Dad!" he yelled out.

As they are getting out of the car, Mother said, "Oh look Franky, there's a little trinket shop. If you want, you may go in and look around, but please don't touch anything."

"WOW! Thanks Mom," Franky said excitedly, as he ran for the door.

Inside the store, Franky saw all kinds of neat stuff. He saw knives, shirts, post cards and souvenirs of every kind. As he slowly wandered through the isles ogling everything and doing his best to not touch as his mother warned, he noticed something interesting on the back wall. He walked over to investigate and found an old dusty display case. As he got closer, he bent down and through the layer of dust, he could see the case held an old Indian spearhead.

"WOW!" he said to himself. "That's neat, I really wish I had that!"

Franky's thoughts of the spearhead were interrupted when he heard his father honking the horn of the car. He took one last glance and ran out of the store to the car.

"Hey guys," exclaimed Franky, "they have the neatest old spearhead in there! I wish I could have it."

"Franky, I bought a little gift for you," Father said.

"For me? What is it?" Franky asked.

"It's a book on the history of the land and our new home. I thought you would like to read about it," said Father. "If you look on page thirty-five you will see a picture of our new house."

"WOW! Dad, This is neat! Thanks!"

Franky turned to the page, and then began to read quietly.

His silence broke as he exclaimed, "Wow! This book tells the story about the Indian village that used to be where our house is now! Mom, you were right! Indians did live on our property!" By now he was really getting excited. There were sure to be many opportunities for exploring, and many new adventures to imagine. Franky poured over his book for the rest of the trip, his imagination was going full speed as the family car toured the countryside. His sister Sarah slept quietly on the seat by him. Neither one of them knew the real life adventure that waited.

After several hours of driving, Mr. Thomas makes the announcement, "Here it is everyone, we're home!" He turned the car into the long, snaking lane that led to the new house.

"Hooray!" shouted Franky, startling Sarah from her peaceful sleep.

Chapter 2

As Father drove further down the lane, Franky was beside himself with excitement. Sarah rubbed the sleep from her eyes and tried to focus on her new surroundings. Franky absorbed every detail noting all the fields, the deep woods, barns and out buildings that he would explore later, there was even a winding creek! At that moment Franky felt he must be the luckiest boy in the world.

In the distance he could see the new house. It had a huge porch with tall white columns and a balcony overlooking the rolling fields, and several huge old trees scattered across the front yard. One tree in particular stood out to Franky. It was a very large oak tree.

"Hmm, That would be a great place to build a treehouse," thought Franky.

With everyone out of the car, Mr. Thomas opened the front door. As everyone stepped into the foyer, their footsteps and voices echoed through the partially furnished rooms. Looking straight ahead was a winding staircase leading up to the second floor.

"Oh look!" exclaimed Mother, "every room has shining wood floors, including the kitchen!" She was very excited as she moved from room to room, because this was the first time she had seen the actual house. She was only shown photos sent to them from her husband's new employer. "And here, the foyer and kitchen windows are stained glass, just like in our church back home! "Oh my! This house is so spacious! I really love this place," mother sang, as she twirled around.

"We certainly won't be rubbing elbows around here," Father chuckled.

Meanwhile, Sarah and Franky went upstairs to pick out their bedrooms.

"OH! I want this one," Sarah exclaimed. This room is so pretty." The room filled with light from the huge bay windows, as the sunlight danced off of the slanted ceiling. The walls were covered with pretty flower printed wallpaper. It was quite a nice room for a little girl.

"You can have it, it's a sissy room with all of those flowers." said Franky grinning.

As he turned to leave, Sarah asked him, "What's this door for, Franky? "Oh man, I bet there's another room behind there Sarah." Just as he reached out to open the door, their father came in.

"Franky! I don't want you, or your sister in that room. There are broken and loose boards in there, and I don't want either of you to get hurt. I will nail it shut tomorrow. In the mean time I want you both to promise not to go in there."

"Okay, we promise," Franky replied, answering for Sarah.

"There are some snacks in the kitchen for you, if you are not too tired to eat and I will be up later to say, good night," Father said.

Franky and Sarah both said, "We are NEVER too tired to eat!" and headed for the kitchen where they seemed to swallow their food whole.

Franky finished first and began to walk back up the stairs to his bedroom. His body was very tired from the drive and the long staircase felt like it would never end. He finally climbed that last step and made it to his room, he looked around and smiled to himself. His mother had made up his bed, as well as put his new book on his pillow. Franky always knew he was lucky to have such great parents, but every day he was reminded of just how much.

He walked over and sat down on his bed. As he reached over to pick up his book, it seemed to fall open to the page that talked about his new house—this house. On that page, there was the photo of his new room! He was so pleased. Franky had a large grin on his face as he looked around and admired his special room. It was then that he first discovered that he even had his very own bathroom.

"No more waiting for Sarah to finish with one of those long bubble baths!" he thought happily.

Franky's room was quite large with built-in bookshelves and storage drawers, a desk and a large closet (where he could hide from Sarah). He even had kerosene lamps hung up high on his walls, (which of course he would check out tomorrow). He laid his book down and went into his bathroom to get ready for bed.

"Wow," this is really cool," he thought excitedly to himself as he looked around. There was a pedestal washbasin with a red and yellow stained glass window above it. In the middle of the window was the figure of a cross. Next to the basin was a really old bathtub with giant feet like lion paws. The commode was the neatest! There wasn't a handle to flush, just a pull chain on the wall. "I know I will really like it here," he thought to himself.

After changing into his pajamas, Franky snuggled into his nice soft bed and resumed reading the history book his father had bought for him. Just then, there was a quiet knock on his door. "Come in" he called, without even looking up from the pages that enchanted him so.

"Just wanted to say goodnight, son." It was his father, "Sarah is already asleep, I don't believe a tornado could wake her tonight," he said, while noticing his sons delight with the book.

"Dad," said Franky, finally breaking away from his reading. "I was just reading in my book how some white men were really cruel and killed the Indians! Why were they so mean?"

"Well son," Father replied, "I don't really know why they were mean to the Indians, except maybe because of greed or jealousy. There are bad people in all races and from all nations, Franky, but there are also a whole lot of good people all over this world too. It's the good examples that are set that we need to follow. We must be thankful that things are better for people today. We must learn from the past, always-treating people with respect regardless of their skin color. It's the person inside that matters most. Do you understand?"

"Yes," replied Franky, "I do understand. My book also tells of how this house has been restored. What exactly does that mean? Did it burn down or something?"

"No," Father chuckled, "that just means that someone remodeled it. They modernized it by putting in updated plumbing, electricity, and things like that, but at the same time keeping it as close to the original look as possible."

"Oh, I get it now," Franky said. "It says here, that this house was built after the Indians were attacked by the white people that hated them, and that only one Indian had survived. It says that the people who did this didn't even live around here."

"Well, son, I know that now a day's when people do bad things, they are motivated by the feeling of power they get by gaining control over another living thing, and maybe it's because they lack any spiritual connection with their Creator or with Nature." "Some people," Father continued, "are so involved in trying to make money that they don't think about the things they destroy, like trees, the Earth, or the people around them."

"Yes, I have seen that with some of my friend's parents at the old house. I'm glad you and Mom are not like that."

"What else does that book of yours say about this old house?" asked Father.

"It says there have been five different families that lived here and that the house was originally built and owned by the Brewer family. It also says," Franky, continued, "that each of the families moved without really telling anyone why. Now that's a mystery to solve if I ever heard one!" Franky said grinning.

"Oh boy, I can see the wheels turning in your head already, Son," Father said laughing. "You go on to sleep now, you'll need your rest in order to investigate all this mystery tomorrow."

"Okay," Franky replied, "Goodnight, Dad."

"Goodnight, Son," Father answered.

Franky snuggled down and began to fall asleep. Just as he was dozing off, he thought he heard something, as he lay listening, he heard the faint call of what sounded like an eagle. Franky knew the eagle's distinct sound from the research he did this year in school through his report about the near extinction of the American Bald Eagle. "How odd, he thought, as he drifted off to sleep.

The night passed quickly, and Franky's dreams were full of exciting things.

Chapter 3

As the sun peeked over the rolling meadows, everyone awoke to the sounds of little Sarah's laughing and giggling. "It's true, it's not a dream, we are really in our new house," Sarah cried with joy.

"Yes, it's really true Sarah," Mother said as she came into Sarah's room. "Now let's get dressed and I'll make our first breakfast in our new home."

Father spoke to them from out in the hall. "Today is a special day, there will no cooking this morning, we are going in town to eat," he said. "My special lady deserves a meal prepared by someone else today—and better for all of us that it be someone other than me!" Father teased.

Mother looked at her husband and smiled saying, "I certainly won't argue with that."

"Franky, Franky," Sarah yelled, as she ran into Franky's room. "Get up, Get up, we're going to town."

"Okay, I'm up," Franky yelled back.

Soon, everyone was washed and dressed and on their way to town. Mother had spotted a quaint little diner on their drive in yesterday and mentioned it to her husband.

"This certainly looks like a friendly place," Mother commented noticing the smiles of the patrons exiting from the restaurant doors.

"I think we will find the whole town to be very friendly," Father replied.

After they were inside and seated, Sarah announced in her usual loud irritating way that she had to go to the bathroom." Oh no," Franky thought as he slouched down in his seat hiding his face. He felt so embarrassed.

"Ok, Sarah, just a minute. What would you like to eat honey?" Father asked his wife."

"Oh, I think I'll have some blueberry pancakes a little bacon and a nice fresh cup of coffee," Mother replied.

"What about you, Sarah?" asked Father pinching her cheek. Sarah pointed to a bright colorful picture on the menu of a plate of bacon, eggs and toast, with orange juice.

"Okay, you two go ahead to the restroom, and I will order your food while you are gone," said Father.

It wasn't until the waitress came to take their order that Franky was able to work up the courage to reappear from behind his menu.

"Hello, little man, are you ready to order?" she asked Franky. "Hmm I haven't seen ya'll in here before. Are you new to the area? Or just passing through?" Without waiting for an answer to her questions, she continued, "Let me guess, I heard someone had bought the old Brewer place, would that be you?"

"Why yes indeed that would be us, we moved in yesterday," Father answered proudly.

"Well now," said the waitress How are you liken' the old castle?"

"The old castle?" Father repeated. "The place is very charming, but a castle? I don't know about that!"

The waitress smiled. "Well just you wait till you get your gas bills, then you'll probably think you are heating an old castle." They both had a good laugh and then, Father placed the order for breakfast.

Once Mother and Sarah returned, the family sat quietly talking and enjoying the peacefulness of the somewhat quiet Sarah. Thanks to the food that had been placed in front of her she was too busy eating to do anything else.

Franky finished eating first. He soon became restless waiting for the others and decided to look around for something to explore. From his seat, he could see a statue of an old Indian over in the corner.

"Dad, can I go over and check out that statue?" Franky asked.

"Sure, son," Father said as he continued to eat.

"Cool," said Franky, as he headed over to the corner. Just as Franky got to the statue, IT MOVED! He nearly jumped out of his skin! The old Indian was real! "Oh, excuse me," mumbled Franky. "Uh, uhm, uh, hi sir, my name is Franky…we just moved here," he stammered. There was no response from the old Indian. "Uh, SIR," said Franky, a little louder.

About that time the waitress called Franky over to her. "Honey, that old man can't see or hear, bless his heart."

"I was beginning to figure that out," said Franky embarrassed.

"Yeah, it's sad, very, very sad, poor thing—he just sits there all day some days…" the waitress continued, as she stared at the old Indian. "I don't think he has said one word since the attack."

"Attack? What attack?" asked Franky.

"Well, not to scare you off or nothing, but a long time ago, before your house was even built, there used to be an Indian village on your land right about where your house sits now. The old Indian lived there with his wife and baby boy. People say that one day while he was hunting, some men rode through the village and slaughtered everyone there, every woman, man, and child. The old Indian's wife and son were among those who were killed."

Franky gasped. "Oh my goodness! I just read about this last night. Do you mean this Indian is the same one they are talking about in my book?"

"Yes," she replied, "one in the same."

"That is so awful! Who could do such an evil thing to another human being?" Franky asked. "Who could do such a horrible thing, especially to women and babies? Did they ever find out who did it?"

"No one knows for sure," the waitress replied. "There's a lot of stories, some say the soldiers; others say it was a group of outlaws. One thing is for sure, whoever did it was not from around here. Everyone in this area owed the Indians their lives."

"Oh really?" inquired Franky. "My book didn't say anything about that. It only mentioned the Indians were murdered and only one survived. Do you know how he got this way?" Franky asked.

"Well, people say that when the old Indian returned to the village and he saw what had happened, he was devastated with grief. He found the body of his wife, Laughing Eyes, but never found the body of Little Star, his son. After searching all night without any sign of his baby boy, his anguish was so great that he told the Spirits he did not want to look upon the beauty of his mother earth, Gia Tulu, or hear the voice of the eagle, with such darkness in his heart."

"WOW, how has he survived all these years? Who took care of him if he couldn't see?" Franky asked in astonishment.

"When the people who lived here heard what happened they rushed to the village and found him as you see him now, except he was wandering in the woods looking for his son. The Brewers were the one's who gave him shelter. They are the same ones who built the house you live in. George Brewer still cares for him now. He's the man who sold the house to your dad."

Franky heard his father calling him. "Franky, come on now, you've bothered her enough with all your questions, it's time to go."

Franky thanked the waitress for her help and headed out the door. It was very strange, but he felt as if he was being watched. He turned to look at the old Indian and could have sworn that he was watching him. "Are those tears on his face?" Franky wondered as he went out the door.

Chapter 4

On the way home Franky was silent, pondering the information that the waitress had told him. He really felt sorry for the old Indian and wanted to become friends with him. "And why did that old Indian seem so familiar to me," Franky thought to himself. This is really turning into a mystery that needs to be investigated.

As Franky stared out the window watching the scenery go by, he begin to daydream about exploring the fields around his house. "Maybe I can find a clue as to what happened to the old Indian's baby."

As he considered this thought, another one popped into his head. "Wow, wouldn't it be neat if I could find some arrowheads or spearheads like the ones at that little store."

"Franky, Franky, stop daydreaming and answer me."

Realizing his mother was talking, Franky said sheepishly, "I'm sorry Mom, what did you say?"

"I want you to watch your sister this afternoon. I have to do some things around the house."

"But I wanted to go exploring today," Franky complained.

"That's fine," his mother said, "but you can take your sister with you."

"Oh, all right," Franky muttered, knowing it would do no good to protest. "Man, what rotten luck," he thought to himself as Sarah made a face at him. "I'm going to be stuck with her all day."

As they got out of the car, he heard his mother saying, "I don't want you and Sarah going too far away, and don't you go running off without your sister. Her legs are a lot shorter than yours are and she can't walk as fast. Be careful now and have fun."

"Yes, Mother, we will! Come on Sarah!" Franky said while reaching for her hand.

"Will you play jump rope with me Franky? Will you, please, please?" Sarah begged.

"Oh, all right, for a little while I guess," Franky answered reluctantly, not really wanting to go along. Sarah went into the garage and in a few minutes reappeared with a rope. She walked over to an old iron post and tied one end to it then gave the other end to Franky.

He began to swing the rope and while Sarah was jumping, Franky slipped into his usual mode of daydreaming. This time he was thinking about the old Indian and what he could do to help him find his baby son. Where could he look, what would he be looking for… Franky deep in thought heard Sarah's screeching voice.

"Hey, you tripped me," she cried.

"No I didn't! You tripped yourself," he told her as he reached out to help her up.

Franky calmed Sarah's crying by changing the subject. "I know Sarah, let's go for a walk in the field." Sarah stopped crying and took Franky's hand and they started walking toward the field. They hadn't gone far before their dad called them.

"Hey you two, lunch will be ready in a few minutes, come and get washed up."

"Okay, coming," yelled Sarah as she broke away from Franky's hand. "You can't catch me," Sarah started singing as she ran toward the house. Just as Franky started to chase her he spotted something shiny in the ground.

"Sarah, wait a minute, Come here!" Franky yelled. "I think I found something!" Sarah turned around and came running back toward Franky."

"What is it, Franky? What is it?"

"I don't know, Sarah, but it looks like gold. Whew, it really is stuck in the ground," he told her as he tried to dig it out with his fingers.

"Franky! Sarah! Come and eat." It was Mother calling them this time. Franky gave the gold thing in the ground a kick with his shoe, then decided he would finish uncovering his discovery after lunch.

"Sarah," he said," let's keep this a secret for now, okay?"

"Okay, I won't tell," Sarah answered, giggling. Meanwhile Franky wondered how to get his father's shovel from the garage and still keep his discovery a secret.

The whole time Franky was washing his hands and face for lunch, his imagination was working overtime. His curiosity was going nuts thinking of all the things this gold piece could be. "I might be rich, that is an awful big nugget," he thought to himself. He dried his hands and face and ran downstairs to the kitchen table. He could barely wait to get finished eating so he could go back to digging up his discovery. Franky took large bites of his sandwich, overstuffing his mouth in an effort to hurry back outside. He was almost finished eating, when Sarah began singing.

"I know a secret, I know a secret!"

This caused Franky to choke on his sandwich. Afraid that Sarah was going to tell about the gold piece, Franky said to her, "Be quiet Sarah it is not polite to sing at the table."

Luckily, Father agreed with him and scolded Sarah and for the moment, the secret was safe. "Whew!" Franky thought, "I'm not going to tell her anything anymore."

"Franky, after lunch, I want you to help me do some chores while your mother and Sarah do some shopping," said Father. Franky sighed a deep sigh of disappointment.

"Okay, sure Dad," he replied, not wanting to appear upset but his mysterious gold piece would have to wait. Most of the time Franky didn't mind at all helping with chores, just not right now. His thoughts and heart was outside in that field. The rest of the day was spent doing chores, just as his father said. Mother and Sarah went off shopping. Franky and his dad cut the grass, trimmed the bushes, and a whole bunch of other odd jobs.

By the time they were finished and cleaned up the mess, it was dinnertime. After dinner, Father went into his study and Mother told Franky and Sarah to go take their bath and get ready for bed.

"Alright, Mom...uh hey, Dad, if you want me to I will help you unpack the garage tomorrow," Franky told his father. He thought this would get him a shovel without drawing attention from his father.

"Well, that would be nice, Franky," said his father, "except I unpacked it earlier today after I fixed the door in Sarah's room. But thanks for offering your help."

"That's okay, I like helping out" Franky said feeling relieved that he wouldn't have to take the extra time tomorrow away from his exploring. Franky and his dad talked a little while longer about the new house, and moving from the old house. This helped Franky to understand a little better the reason why they had to move. "Well, I better go get ready for bed. Good night, Dad."

"Good night, son."

Franky went upstairs to get ready for bed. He stuck his head into Sarah's room on his way down the hall to his room. "Good night, Mom. Night, Sarah."

Sarah and his mom called out, "Good night," to Franky, both at the same time.

"Hey!" he said laughing. "You two singing me a song?"

Franky's head was swimming with a million thoughts about what tomorrow would bring as he uncovered the mysterious gold thing he had found out in the field.

Chapter 5

Morning could not come quick enough for Franky. He kept waking up thinking about the gold piece in the field and wondering what it was. Finally morning came, and as they all sat at the table eating breakfast, Father asked what every one had planned to do for the day. Franky's parents talked about work, shopping and some other stuff.

All Franky could think about was exploring the field. He heard his mother say something about taking Sarah with her when she went into town to the drugstore.

"Good," thought Franky, "I won't have to watch her today, now I can really explore."

"What are your plans for today, Franky?" Father asked.

"I thought I would just snoop around here," he answered beaming. At last his mom and Sarah left and his dad busied himself with hanging pictures and unpacking boxes that still needed to be done.

Franky headed out the door to find the gold piece he saw yesterday. He walked out to where he thought the piece was but did not see it. "Oh no, he exclaimed, "I should have marked the spot where it was. How am I ever going to find it now?"

Franky retraced his steps by walking to the house and back again. He tried hard to remember where he and Sarah were when he first spotted the gold piece. On his third trip, Franky suddenly stopped in his tracks. Overhead, he saw an eagle!

As he looked up in wonder, the eagle circled three times.

Each time the eagle would circle, it called out once. After the third time, the eagle flew away.

"Hmmm, that was kind of weird," Franky muttered to himself. As he went to take another step forward, his foot kicked something in the ground. Franky looked down and there was the gold piece he had been looking for. He stooped down and pulled it out of the ground with his fingers. It came right out, as if it had been waiting for him. He didn't need the shovel after all. Franky brushed the dirt away so he could examine it.

It had a design engraved in it that looked like a spider web. Franky could not contain his excitement any longer.

"Forget about keeping this a secret," he mumbled to himself as he ran as fast as he could back to the house. He called out for his father to come and see what he had found. His father came to the door.

"What is all this commotion about?" he questioned.

Franky ran toward his father shouting, "Dad! Dad! Look what I found!"

"Hey son, that look's like some sort of old Indian medallion. Where did you find it?"

"I found it out in the field!" Franky said excitedly, out of breath.

"Let me take a look at that," Father said as he took hold of Franky's treasure. Turning the piece all around examining it more closely, Father stated, "Son, this looks handmade! I think you have a genuine Indian relic here. Would you like me to clean it up for you?"

"Sure!" Franky replied.

"It may take me a little while to clean this up. I have some stuff in the garage that might help." Franky and his father went out to the garage. Franky's dad carefully sprayed some type of oil on the piece and then wiped it off. Then he turned on a machine that had a round wire type wheel on it. He explained to Franky that the little machine was a wire sander. And, as he held the gold piece up to the wheel, it started to shine in the spot where the wheel touched it. After a few minutes the whole medallion glowed like it was new. After it was cleaned, Father found a strip of leather in an old box of scrap material, attached it to the medallion making a necklace out of it and handed it back to Franky.

"Wow," exclaimed Franky, "this is the neatest thing I have found yet! Do you know what these designs mean?"

"Well," Father said, "it looks like an Indian medallion to me."

"What is it supposed to do?" Franky asked.

"I think the spider web looking part is supposed to catch all the bad dreams and bad energy and trap them in the web until the sun comes out and burns them from the web. "I think the Indians believe that the medallion will protect your spirit and warn you if there is some kind of danger," his father explained.

"This is so cool, I will keep this always," Franky told his father. "Thanks, Dad, for cleaning it up!"

"You're welcome Franky," Father said.

Franky decided to go back outside where he could admire his medallion even better in the sunshine. As he started to leave the garage his thoughts turned back to the old Indian. He was wondering if there was a way to communicate with him. Maybe he could talk to him through his spirit. Maybe his spirit will be his ears and eyes.

As Franky continued to walk toward the door of the garage he noticed that his chest felt like it was vibrating where the medallion touched his skin. It seemed the more he thought about the old Indian the stronger the vibration got. "This is really weird," thought Franky, but before he could mention it to his father, Sarah came running into the garage.

"We're home, we're home," she shouted. "Franky, what's that?" she asked, pointing to the medallion hanging around his neck.

"It's that gold thing I showed you in the field yesterday, and you leave it alone," Franky responded sharply.

"Can I see it? Please!!" Sarah begged. Franky really didn't want to let Sarah touch his new treasure. He was afraid she would lose it or something.

"Franky, let your sister look at it. When she is finished, if you're not going to wear it; take it up to your room and put it away so you don't lose it," his father said.

Franky thought about it a minute, and then finally agreed to let her hold it. He warned her sternly, "Don't drop it. Dad just cleaned it for me."

"Wow!" Sarah said, "it tickles my hand." Sarah looked at the medallion again and then gave it back to Franky, who promptly put it back on his neck.

The rest of the day passed quickly, and soon all were getting settled in for the night. Franky kept the medallion around his neck, taking it off only to take his bath. As he was lying there in bed waiting for sleep to take him over, he could have sworn he heard an eagle calling again. "I wonder if that is the same eagle," Franky thought, as he drifted off to sleep.

Chapter 6

The next morning at breakfast, Franky stated, "I don't think the medallion is working, Dad."

"Why is that?" his father asked.

"I heard crying last night and it woke me up," Franky replied.

"Humph!" Father grunted. "Maybe you had a good dream and forgot."

"Yeah, maybe," laughed Franky.

Mother asked Sarah why she was crying last night. Sarah couldn't remember why or even that she had been crying.

Today everyone, including Sarah, was busy doing the things they wanted to, so that left Franky to enjoy his favorite pastime…daydreaming. In his head, he pictured being with the old Indian, riding on a white horse through town with his medallion shining brightly. His mother's voice brought him out of his dream world and back to reality.

"Come on, kids," called Mother. "We need to go to town to take care of some business. It will be late when we are finished so we will eat dinner in town."

"Can we eat at the diner?" Franky asked her excitedly.

"I think we can, I really like that little place, and they do have good food."

"All right!" Franky said loudly. "Maybe I will get to see the old Indian again," he thought to himself. The excitement that Franky had on the way to town left him as soon as they walked into the diner. Franky looked around and didn't see the old Indian anywhere. His disappointment must have shown, because when the waitress who had talked to him before about the Indian was approaching their table she noticed his sad face, and ask him what was the matter.

"Well," replied Franky, "I really wanted to see the old Indian today."

"Don't be so sad Franky, He'll be here soon. He's here regular as clockwork every day, right after he performs the ceremonial dance to honor the spirits and the Creator." About that time the door opened and in walked the Indian, escorted by George Brewer.

Franky finished eating quickly and asked if he could go talk to the old Indian. His father gave his permission but reminded Franky that the old man probably tires out easily, so don't become a bother.

Franky's heart was beating so hard he thought it would come out of his chest as he approached the Indian. "Hello," Franky said, as he got close to the old Indian. "I know that you can't hear or see me, but I was kind of hoping that your spirit would be your eyes and ears. I brought something to show you."

Franky took the medallion he had found and put it in the hand of the old Indian, and begin to tell him how he found it. Franky was explaining to him how when he went back to look for the shiny gold piece the second time he couldn't find it, and how he believes an eagle helped him from the sky.

It was at that moment he noticed a change in the old Indian's expression. Franky begin to feel a shield of energy around him and the Indian. It was like a warm golden colored breeze. This was a new experience for him. Suddenly the old Indian was shaking so fast he was vibrating. He looked toward Franky's face and this time Franky could see clearly that a tear was running down the old man's cheek.

Just then Franky heard his father beeping the car horn. He knew that he must leave. And so he gently took the medallion from the wrinkled hand of the old Indian and promised faithfully to come back and visit with him again.

Chapter 7

On the way home Franky let Sarah play with the medallion. Sarah put it around her neck and kept asking everyone if she was pretty. She was not satisfied until her mother, father and Franky had told her that she was. Franky's thoughts remained on the old Indian. He couldn't shake the feeling that somehow he knew him.

About halfway home Sarah fell asleep. The rest of the way home Franky remained lost deep in his thoughts. Later, as he crawled into bed he remembered that Sarah still had his medallion, but he was too tired to get out of bed to get it from her.

Once again, in the silence, just before slumber he thought he heard an eagle's call. "How odd," he thought as he fell asleep.

Franky had been asleep for what seemed like just a few minutes, when Sarah's screaming woke him up. His father and mother both went running to her room.

"Mommy, get the baby, the baby is hurt, you have to find it," Sarah cried.

Mother held her in her arms, "It's okay, honey, you are only dreaming."

Franky shuffled into the room. "What's wrong with Sarah?" he asked sleepily.

"It's alright, she just had a bad dream, go back to bed," said his father.

Just then Franky noticed that Sarah had the medallion on. "I guess your theory about the medallion really was wrong, Dad. Even with it Sarah still had a bad dream."

Father took the dream web and handed it to Franky, and with a stern look, "GOOD NIGHT, son." Franky took it, chuckling, and went back to bed. As Franky lay in bed, he began to think about the old Indian. Holding the medallion reminded him about the change that occurred when the old Indian touched it today. And he also remembered the tears on his face.

"I know he can communicate. I just know it," he said, pulling up his blanket.

The next morning Sarah did not remember having a bad dream and questioned why she was in her parent's bed. They explained that she was restless and this seemed to satisfy her.

Franky, on the other hand, felt sad today. He thought that the medallion would have made the Indian smile, not cry. He hoped the Indian knew how sorry he was, and that he didn't mean to upset him.

"Franky," called Father, interrupting his thoughts, "I'm going to need your help today so don't run off anywhere."

"Okay," he answered." What are we going to do?"

"Today I am going to show you how to paint," his father told him.

"Cool! That is so cool!" Franky jumped up out of bed and dressed quickly almost tripping on his untied shoelace as he tried to hurry.

"Slow down," Father said laughing. "Let's eat breakfast first."

They all sat down to eat. Franky was so excited he could hardly sit still.

Chapter 8

Finally everyone was done eating and Father told Franky to come on as he headed toward the door. Franky's curiosity was really starting to get the best of him. Father had not yet told him what they were going to paint.

"What are we going to paint?" ask Franky.

"Well, come on and I'll show you," his father replied. Franky really got excited when he realized they were going to the shed that Father had told him not to go in.

His father opened the door to the shed and there sitting on some saw horses was a real Indian canoe.

"Dad," Franky said almost in a whisper, "is this what we are going to paint?"

"Yep, it is," said Father, then he chuckled at the awe in his son's voice.

"First, we have to sand it real smooth and then we'll paint it." Father got the sandpaper and showed Franky the difference in the roughness of the sandpaper, then he explained which to use first. He picked the sanding block up and showed Franky how to use it. He instructed him to sand the same direction as the grain of the wood on the canoe.

Franky tried the sanding block and under the watchful eye of his father he became pretty good at sanding in a short time. Father felt sure that Franky would be all right alone for a few minutes and left him to go to the house for something to drink. Franky was feeling real proud that his father trusted him enough to leave him alone with such an important job. However, he was not sanding too long before his famous imagination took him over and in an instant he was down by the river with the canoe.

In his mind he could picture the river, the trees and even the bright sunshine up above. He imagined himself dressed in red breach cloth and tan leather leggings. He had a bearskin over his shoulder and an eagle feather in his hair. It was kind of angled to the side. Franky knew that you were not supposed to wear a feather straight up in the air because that was considered dishonorable. The canoe looked a little different also, but Franky didn't really have time to think about the differences in the canoe because a very large bear had come up behind him and started to speak to him.

The bear was talking about who Franky was and he told Franky that the medicine was to be his, as long as he was honorable and did not misuse the power the medicine would give him. As the great bear spoke, Franky thought how strange it was that he could understand the him.

The bear continued to speak and told him not to wonder about understanding. The large bear told Franky that he was part of nature and all of nature could talk to each other. He told Franky that at one time all humans could communicate with all of nature. It wasn't until greed, jealousy, and selfishness robbed them of the gift that kijii wasii monato (Great Good Spirit), the Creator, had given them.

"Franky! Franky!" The vision of the bear suddenly transformed into his sister Sarah and she was shaking his shoulders. "Is this your boat? Does it have a name?" Sarah asked.

Franky looked around and saw he was back in the shed. He tried to explain to his sister the difference between a boat and a canoe, but it was no use, she just could not see the difference.

Franky had finished one half of the canoe and leaned over to look at the other side when his medallion hit the canoe. He didn't want to scratch the canoe or his dream web so he took it off and hung it on a nail. Franky was concentrating so intently on the job of sanding that he failed to notice that Sarah had taken it when she left.

In a little while his father came back with two lemonades. "Hey, Franky, come take a break," he said as he offered Franky a cold lemonade. "You're doing a fine job on the canoe son, I'm real proud of you. I knew you could do it." Franky took the lemonade and sipped it slowly. "I'll help you finish sanding it after we finish our lemonade," Father told him. Franky was proud of himself and feeling pretty good about the praise his father had given him. He had really tried hard to do a good job.

As the two of them stood back and admired the work Franky had done, Father remarked how the canoe was starting to look like brand-new. He told him again what a good job he had done on it.

Chapter 9

"It's getting close to dinnertime now," said Father. "We better clean up." They finished cleaning up the mess from all the sanding they had done and started back to the house. As Franky walked with his father, his head was swollen with pride. Franky was so busy planning his adventures on the river with the canoe he forgot all about grabbing his special medallion from the nail.

While they were eating their dinner Father commented to his wife, "Hon, you would have been real proud of Franky today, he really worked hard on the canoe. Done a fine job too."

"Well, I'm glad to hear that," said his mother. "It's nice to hear good things about you Franky, instead of hearing how much trouble you get into because of all your daydreaming."

Franky was still smiling to himself that evening as he was getting ready for bed. He had no trouble falling asleep, and when he did the smile was still on his face.

All was quiet when his mother and father retired to their room. Mother and father drifted off to sleep, however, the quiet didn't last.

Soon everyone was awakened by little Sarah's screams. Father, Mother and Franky all jumped out of bed and ran down the hall to Sarah's room. As they entered the room, Sarah cried, "Please Mommy, help the baby. The baby is crying, it's hurt, please, Mommy, get the baby."

"Shhhh, Sarah, it's all right," Mother said, as she picked Sarah up and tried to calm her.

"Sarah, wake up," Father said softly. "It is only a dream, wake up sweetheart."

Franky stood in the doorway watching his parents comfort Sarah when he noticed his special medallion lying on Sarah's bed. Franky was surprised that he hadn't missed it. His mother gave Franky back his medallion necklace and told him to go back to bed. "You go on back to bed too dear," she said to her husband. "I'll stay with Sarah until she falls back to sleep."

"I won't argue with that," he answered, "but I will wait up for you."

"All right dear," Mother said smiling to herself. She knew her husband would be asleep as soon as his head hit the pillow.

Mother rocked Sarah until she was asleep, then put her back in bed and tucked her in. She went back to her bedroom and found Father just as she had thought—sound asleep. She kissed her husband gently on his cheek before getting back into bed herself. Soon everyone was asleep again.

The next morning, Mother and Father had a private conversation in the dining room concerning Sarah's bad dreams.

"I am really concerned about Sarah," said Mother.

"Yes, I am too," Father replied, "and it seems to be the same dream each time."

"Perhaps we should take her in town to see the doctor," Mother suggested.

"Good idea, let me know when her appointment is and I'll go with you," agreed Father.

"Okay," answered Mother, "I'll call this morning."

Father went outside and found Franky sitting on the steps. "What are you thinking about with such a serious look on your face?" his father asked.

"I was just thinking about Sarah" Franky replied.

"Don't worry. I'm sure she will be just fine. Now, let's go take another look at the ole' canoe."

As they walked to the shed, Franky's father suggested to him that he should give the canoe a proper name. All fine vessels should indeed have a name.

Franky wondered why his father wanted him to name the canoe. His thoughts were interrupted by his father's voice, "I'm giving the canoe to you, Franky. So give it a special name, one that has meaning."

"You are giving it to me!" exclaimed Franky. "Wow, that's cool, thanks Dad." Franky ran over and gave him a big hug.

Franky was grinning from ear to ear as they entered the shed. He had already thought of a special name for his canoe. "I'm going to name my canoe, 'The Old Indian,'" Franky announced to his father.

"Well now, son, that sounds like a proper name. It seems that Indian at the diner made quite an impression on you."

Just then Sarah came into the shed, "Daddy, Mommy says to come in—we have to go into town now."

"All right, Sarah, run along, I'll be right there," Father told her. After Sarah left Franky asked his father where they were going. "Oh, we are taking Sarah to the doctor for a checkup."

"Do I have to go?" asked Franky, secretly hoping that he wouldn't.

After thinking about it for a moment his father said, "I think you are old enough to stay here by yourself for a few hours. But, don't wander off anywhere, agreed?"

"Agreed," promised Franky. "Maybe I'll read a book or something."

Father chuckled. "Son, where you are concerned, it's the 'or something' that worries me."

Franky smiled and waved goodbye to his family. He couldn't help feeling that he was all grown up.

Chapter 10

Looking up at the blue sky he thought about how beautiful the day was.

"Hmm, what kind of bird is that up there so high? Is that an eagle?" Franky said to himself. He watched it for a while, but still was not able to make out what kind of bird it was, and then with a blink of an eye it was gone.

Franky grabbed a blade of grass to chew on and lay down under the big oak tree. Suddenly, he sat up as he remembered the kerosene lamps he wanted to check out. But with a second thought, he decided that he was too tired to bother with them right now.

Franky laid back and closed his eyes to enjoy the warm sunshine and fresh air. He began feeling something really weird. Suddenly he felt as if the tree and the ground were absorbing him. It felt almost like he was becoming part of everything around him. Franky had never felt anything quite like this before. It was a pleasant feeling, and felt like pure love. He felt like he was floating among the stars.

Finally, Franky opened his eyes and looked around, and to his bewilderment he saw nothing but trees everywhere. His house was gone. His clothes were completely different. He was wearing tan buckskin leggings, a red breach cloth and moccasins—just like in his vision! Franky was still in a fog when he began to smell a campfire in the air. He walked toward the scent thinking that someone there might be able to explain what was happening to him.

He had not gone very far, when someone grabbed him by the shoulders and shook him. He was getting scared when he heard his name, "Franky, Franky, wake up." his sister Sarah was saying. Franky slowly opened his eyes to see his father standing before him.

"Hey there, are you being lazy and taking a nap?" ask Father teasingly.

Franky yawning looked up and nodded his head.

"Son, did you build a fire while we were gone?" Father asked, with a puzzled look on his face. "I smell smoke. Can you smell it?"

About that time they heard an eagle call. They all looked up just in time to see three lightning bolts flash.

"Humph, now that's odd," Father commented. "There is not a cloud in the sky, I hope that is not what I smell, a fire could have started somewhere in the field from them bolts."

Dinner was extra special that night. Franky felt different than he did when he woke up that morning. He seemed to appreciate his family and his new home more.

He could not get the memory from his mind of what had happened earlier beneath the old oak tree. He felt so good that he was extra nice to Sarah, and offered to play her favorite game after dinner. "How was Sarah's checkup today?" Franky asked.

"That was nice of you, Franky, to ask about your sister," said Mother. She then continued on with "The doctor said there was nothing wrong physically, but the move here could be the cause of her nightmares. He suggested that we stay with her in her room instead of taking her to ours though. He said it would probably help her to get adjusted to the change and still make her feel safe."

"Well, I am glad that Sarah is all right, I was worried about her, even though she gets on my nerves once in awhile." Franky said. "May I be excused now? I would like to read some before I go to bed."

"Yes, you may, and be sure to take a bath and brush your teeth," his mom replied. His mother watched him as he went toward the steps. She was smiling to herself thinking about how handsome he was getting and how grown up he seemed all of a sudden.

Franky went up to his room and got ready for bed, taking his bath and brushing his teeth. As he lay down with his book, he double-checked to make sure that he had his medallion and not Sarah. Franky was not really a selfish person, but he did not want his little sister to break or lose his new treasure. He thought it might be valuable, and he also liked the vibration he felt sometimes whenever he touched it.

The next morning Franky woke up to the smell of bacon cooking. He heard his mother in the kitchen humming to herself and wondered why she was so happy. He got up and washed his face and hands then headed downstairs to eat, feeling excited about the thought of exploring all day.

"Good morning, Mom," said Franky. "Is there anything I can do to help?"

"Nope, everything is pretty much ready, why don't you take a seat over there and I'll fix you a plate," she said, and then continued to hum.

Finally, Franky asked her why she was so happy.

"Well, I am surprised you did not notice your sister slept all night. She never woke up—not one time. In fact she is still asleep!" Mother told him.

His mother continued to dish up the food on everyone's plate. She suggested that Franky go up to check on his sister to see if she was waking yet. Franky ran upstairs, and as he started to enter Sarah's room he heard her stirring, so he just hollered, "Come on Sarah, breakfast."

In just a few minutes Sarah and his father came in and sat down. Mother asked for the blessing on the food and they all enjoyed their breakfast. As they were eating, Sarah talked about her dolls and Father was commenting on how Mother was the best bacon maker around. The rest of breakfast seemed to fly by, and soon Franky was headed outside to explore.

Franky explored and examined almost every inch of the fields except the area down by the creek. Father had specifically told him not to go there alone.

Franky could almost see where the old village had stood and all the wigwams that were there. He imagined that he smelled the cook fires of the Indians that lived on this land. These thoughts made him think of the old Indian at the little diner in town and how badly he must miss his family. He could not understand why people would want to hurt other people, especially women and little babies. Franky was thinking of how much he would miss his family if something were to happen to them when he came up to the old oak tree and decided to take a rest.

Chapter 11

At the same time Franky sat down beneath the old oak tree, he heard an eagle call. He looked up and saw what seemed to be the same eagle from the other day. Franky thought how odd it was that he only seemed to see the eagle here. He leaned back against the old oak tree, and as he closed his eyes he felt the same light floating sensation he had felt the other day coming over him.

Once again, he was becoming part of all nature. The floating sensation felt so relaxing. It was like having his mother's arms wrapped around him while she rocked him to sleep.

All at once Franky woke up. When he looked around he realized he was in the deep woods just like before.

His house was gone, there were so many trees he could not count them, and once again he smelled a campfire. He looked at his clothes and sure enough he was dressed like an Indian. He had on the same leather leggings, red breach cloth and moccasins. He also saw his medallion hanging from the leather strap around his neck. The only difference was it seemed to glow and vibrate with energy.

"This is an awesome dream," Franky thought to himself. He looked through the trees and could see the Indian village. Of course, being Franky, he had to explore it. As he started to walk toward the village, an Indian man about ten years older than he came through the trees.

The Indian said to Franky, "There you are Little Cougar, your grandfather asked me to keep you out of mischief and to begin teaching you of the medicine ways of our people."

Even though Franky understood what was being said, he knew that it was not in English. Franky asked the Indian who he was. The Indian laughed, and said, "you are always playing, Little Cougar, but it is time to be serious nephew. You know I am Walking Bear, your uncle." Although Franky had never heard anyone refer to him by an Indian name, Little Cougar, it felt and sounded absolutely right.

Walking Bear, the uncle, began to explain to Franky how the animals and the humans are all related, and how we are all apart of the trees and everything that is around us.

"All things are a part of us and we are a part of all things," Walking Bear said. He told Franky that when we injure or abuse the trees, animals or our mother, Gia Tula (the Earth or Nature), we do these things to ourselves and to our Creator whom they called "M'Sum8a" or Grandfather.

"Some of the white humans referred to the Grandfather as God or Father. Some call him Jehovah," Walking Bear told "Little Cougar." He went on that the Indian peoples sometimes referred to the Creator as Kijji Wasii Manoto, which meant Great Good Spirit. Walking Bear explained that not all spirits are good, and that we do not want any of the bad spirits to come to us.

Franky did not know how long they had been walking and talking, but he was having fun and learning so much. Suddenly, Walking Bear stopped speaking and just stood there listening. He turned to Franky and very sternly told him to stay there until he came back. Franky was very confused as he watched Walking Bear running toward the village. Franky being the curious young boy that he was, tried to follow Walking Bear at a distance, but alas, Walking Bear seemed to disappear. To Franky's horror, he heard Walking Bear cry out in anguish.

Franky began calling to Walking Bear, trying to go toward the village but something grabbed his shoulders and shook him.

Chapter 12

"Wake up," Father said. "Franky, you are going to sleep past dinner." Franky opened his eyes and looked around. Dazed, he wondered, "How in the world did I get here?" Franky was in his own bed, in his own room. Quickly he washed his face and went down to eat.

"Tomorrow is the big day," Father said as he put another spoonful of food in his mouth. "Yep, tomorrow Franky will put the final touches on his canoe, by painting the new name he has chosen on it."

"Oh! What name is that?" asked his mother.

"The Old Indian," Franky announced proudly. "I chose that name because when I look at the canoe I can almost see the old Indian from the diner sitting in it."

Franky was still wondering about his dream and how he got from the tree to his bed.

"I think that it's a great name for the canoe, Franky. Now finish your dinner, it's getting late and you both need to get your bath so you can get ready for bed," Mother said, as she began clearing the table of dirty dishes. Franky excused himself from the table and went to get ready for his bath.

About an hour later Franky's mother headed upstairs to get a book from her bedroom, she noticed that Franky's light was still on. She went to check on him and found that he had fallen asleep in the tub. She smiled to herself and went out and had her husband come upstairs to wake him. She knew it would really embarrass Franky if she woke him.

The sun rose at six a.m. and Franky was up with it. He was excited about painting the canoe, as well as the possibility of putting it in the water today. When Franky walked into the kitchen, both his parents called out good morning almost at the same time, and Franky responded with a hearty good morning of his own. Mother was talking to Father about how Sarah had gone two nights without a bad dream.

"I guess the doctor was right," Mother said. "It must have been the move, and her needing to get adjusted to her new surroundings." Father agreed with her and asked where Sarah was.

Franky had just sat down at the table when Sarah came in tiredly rubbing her eyes. As they were eating breakfast, Franky's parents discussed their plans for the day and what needed to be accomplished. After breakfast Franky and his dad headed toward the shed that housed the canoe. Franky was kind of nervous and a little bit afraid that he would make a mistake and mess up his beautiful canoe.

"You'll do just fine, I know you will Franky," his dad said confidently. "Just take your time." His dad outlined the name Franky had picked on both sides of the canoe, then stood up and said, "There, now all you have to do is to paint inside the outline that I have drawn and everything will look just fine. I think you might be able to work better if you don't have me looking over your shoulder," he said as he turned to go back to the house.

After his dad left, Franky sat and stared at the blank lettering. Finally, he took a deep breath and picked up the paintbrush and began to paint. Franky was focusing so intently on what he was doing, he was done before he realized it. He took a step back away from his canoe and was admiring his work. He was so focused on every detail of the job he had just finished that he didn't hear his father come up behind him.

When his dad spoke, Franky almost jumped out of his skin, which of course made Father laugh out loud.

"I didn't mean to scare you, son," his dad chuckled. "Franky, I must say you have done a really good job. Are you hungry? How about we go up to the house and get a snack." Franky responded with a big smile and an "okay." Franky was very proud of himself and his head swelled a little because of the bragging his dad had been doing over him lately.

Just as they got to the house, Sarah and his mom pulled into the driveway. Franky had been so involved in painting the letters he had not realized they had even left.

His dad waved hello to his wife and daughter. As he was gathering a couple of bags of groceries from the back seat, he proceeded to tell his wife what a great job Franky had done on the canoe. His father's comments of course, made Franky's head swell even more with pride.

"That's great Franky, I'm real proud of you," Mother said. She gave Franky a big hug and smiled, then told them all to wash up because she had bought hamburgers from the diner.

"The diner—" Franky said. "Did you see the old Indian?" He was hoping for a yes.

"No, honey, I'm sorry I didn't see him."

"Oh, okay," Franky muttered disappointedly, grabbed a bag of groceries and headed for the house. Before Franky began to wash the paint off of his hands and face, he took the medallion off and laid it on the shelf above the toilet. He promptly finished washing and ran downstairs to eat the hamburgers his mother had brought. He completely forgot about the medallion that was still on the shelf where he had put it.

Since their father was in the downstairs bathroom washing up, Sarah went into Franky's bathroom to wash her hands.

As she walked into the bathroom, she immediately spotted the medallion. She picked it up and took it to her room and put on her doll's neck. Smiling at how pretty the necklace looked on her dolly, she returned to the bathroom to wash her hands.

Everyone was eating and laughing with Father, still talking about the great job Franky had done, not just on the letters, but the whole canoe. Franky was starved, and very busy shoving his hamburger into his mouth, while he listened intently to his father brag about him. Not one thought entered Franky's mind about his medallion. Franky was grinning so much that his cheeks started to hurt.

"After we are finished can we take the canoe out to the river, Dad?" Franky asked.

"No, Franky, I'm sorry, I have to make some phone calls. Maybe this weekend we will get to do that."

Although Franky was a little disappointed that he did not get to take his canoe out, he understood. His father had to earn a living and needed to make those phone calls. With Father working in his study and Mother tending to Sarah, Franky decided he would go to bed a little earlier than normal so he could read his book.

As he glanced through his book, Franky wondered if there were alligators in the river. (Of course this one thought was all it took to activate Franky's imagination.)

Franky saw himself dressed as Little Cougar down by the river pushing his canoe into the water. All of a sudden a great alligator grabbed the canoe. Franky picked up his spear and began to fight with the ferocious beast. They fought for what seemed like hours. The great battle stopped when he heard two cries from an eagle and saw lightening flash three times in the bright blue sky. The alligator swam off and Franky thought the eagles would never be quiet again. It kept calling and calling and screaming and screaming.

Suddenly, Franky woke up with a start. That scream was from his sister; she was having a bad dream again.

Sarah was crying, "The baby, Mommy, the baby is hurt, get the baby Mommy, the baby is crying, get the baby Mommy."

Chapter 13

Franky ran into Sarah's room. His mother and father were already in there. His mother was holding Sarah, trying to calm her down.

"Go back to bed, son," Father said. "It's all right."

Franky went back to bed and Mother let Sarah finish the night in her and Father's bed, even though it was against the doctor's advice. The rest of the night passed with no more bad dreams.

The next morning at breakfast, Mother and Father decided that if the bad dreams came again, one of them would sleep with Sarah to see if that would better help her. They couldn't understand why she was having the dreams again. Sarah came wandering sleepily into the kitchen, seemingly unaware of the past night's bad dream.

"Why was I sleeping in your bed, Mommy?" Sarah asked.

"You had another bad dream honey, and we thought you might sleep better in our bed with us," Mother said as Sarah climbed up on her lap.

Franky listened as his parents talked to Sarah, trying to figure out why she was having these nightmares. Even though Franky was listening, he was thinking about all the preparation that had to be done before they could ever launch his canoe. Father had told Franky that he must cut all the weeds down to clear a path to the river. With a warning to "be careful" Franky headed for the shed to find the weed cutter. He was very eager to take his canoe out on the water.

Franky worked hard all day long, stopping only long enough to eat the peanut butter and jelly sandwich and apple his mom had made for his lunch. He cut and trimmed weeds and brush and hauled them up to the back yard for his father to burn later. With every load of brush Franky brought up the hill to his yard, he seemed to become more excited, knowing he was that much closer to launching his canoe. Finally everything was ready.

Mother was calling for him to come in for dinner. Franky couldn't believe how quickly the day had passed. Franky was very proud of himself for getting everything ready to launch his canoe. It wasn't until after dinner that he realized how tired he was. Franky sat in the living room trying to watch his favorite television program, but his eyes kept going shut. He thought to himself, "This is silly to fight sleep so hard, I'm going to bed." He got up walked over kissed his mother and father and Sarah goodnight. "See you all in the morning," Franky said as he started up the steps. Franky had been so busy all day cleaning up the weeds, that he didn't think even one time about his medallion, or the old Indian. "Man," Franky thought, "I don't think I have ever worked that hard." He was right on the verge of sleep when he heard the familiar calling of the eagle. It was somehow comforting to hear the eagle, and Franky drifted into a sound sleep.

The house was quiet until a familiar but unwelcome sound woke everyone up.

"Mommy! Mommy! The baby, get the baby Mommy, it's hurt, please Mommy, get the baby!" It was Sarah with another one of her dreams.

Franky didn't even bother getting out of bed this time, he just pulled his pillow over his head and tried to go back to sleep.

"You stay in bed dear, I'll go to her," Mother said to her husband. "Shhh," Mother said as she went into Sarah's room, "Wake up honey, you are dreaming, it's alright it was only a dream. I'll stay with you in your bed tonight," her mom told her. Soon they were cuddled together and sound asleep. A short time later Mother began to dream, she dreamt that she heard an eagle calling. But, there was something different about the call of the eagle. She was hearing another sound, other than just the calling eagle. It sounded like a baby crying. Mother's eyes popped open and she sat straight up. She was wide-awake and she still heard the baby crying. At first she thought it was Sarah, but soon realized that the cry she was hearing was a baby not a six-year-old. As Mother looked down she saw that Sarah was crying too. Soon her cries turned to screams. Mother was a bit spooked, so she quickly scooped Sarah up in her arms and ran to her own bedroom. Although her husband did not wake up as her and Sarah got into bed with him, she still felt safe and secure beside him. After tossing and turning a while, Mother was finally able to go back to sleep. She woke up early and went down to make coffee, still upset about what had happened the night before.

Chapter 14

Father came into the kitchen, "I thought I smelled fresh coffee," he said. He walked over to hug his wife and as he turned her around he saw that she had been crying. "Hey, what's wrong? Are you sick, you're pale as a ghost."

"A ghost is just what I think it is," said Mother. She began to tell him about the eagles and the baby crying. "At first, I thought it was Sarah, but then I realized the sound I was hearing was an infant, not a six-year-old.

Dad chuckled, and held her tighter, and explained that she probably was sleeping lightly and was hearing Sarah cry, because when you dream, things can be all mixed up and seem like it's real.

"We don't have any babies around here, unless there is something you never told me," Father said as he playfully tickled Mother.

Mother shook her head and said," No, I know what I heard. I heard a baby and it wasn't Sarah."

"Aw, come on hon, you don't really believe in all that ghost stuff. I'm sure it was just a dream."

Mother laughed a little at this point and told him he was probably right, about it being only a dream. She kissed him on the cheek and told him to sit down and she would get him some coffee and breakfast.

Father was glad that she was feeling better, but in the back of his mind he was a little concerned. He had never seen his wife this upset and scared about anything before.

The day came and went with everyone busy doing things. Sarah played with her dolls, and Mother worked around the house still trying to shake the feeling she had from the night before. Father and Franky worked outside all day putting in the garden. They all spent the evening gathered around the kitchen table going through a box of old photos Dad had found in the garage. It was a pleasant evening and there was no talk of the nightmares. Before long, it was bedtime for Franky and Sarah.

After tucking her daughter into bed, Mother returned to the living room to work on her crocheting and she finished watching a movie on TV. About halfway through the movie, she became sleepy and decided to join her husband who was already snoring in the upstairs bedroom.

Laying down, Mother found she could not sleep, even though she was tired. She tossed and turned. "I think I'll go in bed with Sarah, maybe she'll be able to sleep through the night," she thought to herself.

As she started to crawl in bed with Sarah, she noticed Franky's medallion lying on the pillow. "I better keep this for Franky," she thought as she slipped the medallion around her neck. I'll give it to him in the morning."

She then snuggled down under the covers with Sarah and eventually dozed off. She was asleep for only a short time when Sarah woke her up crying. It was a repeat of the night before. Complete with the sound of the infant crying.

"This is crazy, I am a grown woman, I will not be afraid of this room." She decided to put Sarah in the guestroom; because there was no need for both of them to lose sleep over this dream or ghost or whatever it was. "I'm going to deal with this thing once and for all," she thought to herself.

Mother's plan was to stay awake to see if she could see anything.

Even though she tried very hard to stay awake, sleep eventually took over and she drifted off.

Father was suddenly awakened by the sound of his wife crying. At first he was confused, not knowing where she was, but soon realized she was in Sarah's room and went down the hall to find out what was wrong. He was surprised as he entered the room to find her sitting up with her arms reaching out as if trying to pick up a baby, she was crying saying, "Hush little one I'm here, it will be all right, I'm coming."

Father shook her. "Wake up, honey, wake up. You're having another nightmare."

His wife opened her eyes and started telling him about the nightmare she was having. It was no different than the ones before.

He stroked her hair and held her tight as she continued to sob, trying to explain. "It was NOT just a dream! The baby was real, the blanket was red and yellow striped, and it was a real baby crying. I know it wasn't Sarah, because I put her to bed in the guestroom. It is something in this room.

Mother was sobbing in her husband's arms as he held her and tried to comfort her. He was not really sure what to say. He didn't have a good explanation about the nightmares. "Why is Sarah in the guest room?" Father asked.

"I put her in there so that at least one of us could get a decent night's sleep. Then I came back in here to prove to myself that all this nonsense was being caused by the fear of new places in the mind of a six-year-old. As it turned out," Mother continued, "it isn't just Sarah, *It is this room!"*

Father reached out and gave her another hug, then noticed that she was wearing Franky's medallion."

"Are you the big chief?" he asked jokingly, trying to cheer her up. Mother kind of chuckled, starting to feel a little sheepish at being so scared.

"No, Sarah had it. I was going to give it to Franky in the morning." She removed it from around her neck and laid it on the table beside the bed. Her husband put his arms around her and gave her a gentle little hug.

"What do you say we go to our room and try to get some sleep? We can talk about all this in the morning. Maybe we can figure something out then."

She was very thankful that her husband was such a kind and gentle man. They both stood up and walked hand in hand down the hall to their room. Mother slept with her head on father's chest the rest of the night with no more interruptions.

Chapter 15

At breakfast Franky's dad was reading the morning paper, when from behind the paper, Franky heard him say, "Hey, there's a circus in town!" He put the paper down and looked right at Sarah and Franky. "How would the two of you like to go to the circus tonight? In fact, why don't we make it an all day affair?"

"That's a great idea!" exclaimed Franky's mother. "Why don't we pack a picnic lunch and explore that cute little park I saw when we first got here?" asked his mom.

"Okay," said his dad, "and we'll grab some dinner at the diner before the circus. Franky, maybe you'll get to see your Indian friend!"

"Yeah!" yelled Franky jumping up out of his chair. The thought of the opportunity to see his Indian friend really pleased Franky. He ran up the steps taking them two at a time to go get ready.

"A circus, a circus, we're going to the circus," Sarah sang, clapping her little hands together in time to her singing.

"Honey, would you mind packing the picnic lunch while I get Sarah cleaned up?" Mother asked.

"Sure, no problem," her husband replied. Sarah and her mom went upstairs and Franky's dad cleared the table of the breakfast dishes, got out the picnic basket and began filling it with sandwiches, chips, cookies and some fruit. He threw in a few cans of pop to finish it all off. The whole house was bustling with excitement, and before long they were all and headed into town.

They explored every inch of the park, and discovered a hiking trail and a very cool playground. Franky and his father played catch for a little while with the ball Franky brought from home. Sarah and her mother had a good time swinging on the swings and playing in the sandbox.

Soon it was lunchtime and they all helped to get everything ready. Sarah spread out the checkered tablecloth, Franky laid out the paper plates, napkins and plastic forks. Mother dipped some potato salad onto their plates and passed out the sandwiches and chips. Father filled the plastic cups with ice and poured the cans of pop into them.

After lunch, Franky's dad surprised him and Sarah with a kite. While Sarah, Franky and their dad played with the kite, Franky's mother cleaned up the table, then sat on a blanket under a tree and read a book.

It was a wonderful day, and all thoughts of the nightmares went away for a while. The afternoon passed by quickly and the sun started to go down.

"We better get going if we're going to eat at the diner before going to the circus," Franky's dad announced. With that, everyone helped gather their things and loaded them into the car and they were off to the diner.

Franky was filled with excitement. "Maybe the old Indian will be there so I can talk to him again," Franky thought.

They arrived at the diner and Franky was the first out of the car and into the diner. His dad followed close behind him. Sarah and her mother brought up the rear. Upon entering the diner, Franky quickly scanned the place and mumbled, "Darn."

"Did you say something, Franky?" asked his father.

"Oh, I was hoping he would be here, but he's not." Franky said.

Franky's dad knew exactly who the "he" was that Franky was talking about without even asking. "Well, don't worry, I'm sure we will be back here another time, eventually we will run into him again."

"Yeah, I know, I'm just a little disappointed that's all," Franky replied.

The conversation around the table was lively and full of talk about what they might see at the circus. Franky tried to hide his disappointment about not getting to see his Indian friend, but inside he was very sad. They finished eating, and Dad paid the bill while Franky, Sarah and their mom got into the car. The circus was being held in an open lot not very far from the diner, and the drive there was short. They all went in and the usher showed them where their seats were located. They all laughed and clapped, and thoroughly enjoyed each and every part of the circus. Franky and Sarah had the time of their lives. Sarah sat on her father's shoulders so she could see the entire clown acts and animal tricks.

Franky ate so much cotton candy he felt like he would burst.

This was a most perfect day, Franky and Sarah were sad to see it end, but it did and every one went back to the car.

The drive home was quiet and peaceful, Franky and Sarah fell asleep, being exhausted from the day's activities. Mother sat close to Father leaning on his shoulder.

Father gently kissed her on the forehead and asked if she felt all right and if she had a good time. He pretty much knew the answer, but could sense that something was bothering her.

"Yes, it was a wonderful day…I'm kind of dreading going home," she answered, and then continued, "Do you believe in spirits or ghosts?"

Father laughed, trying to make light of the question, and said, "Casper, the friendly kind."

"I'm serious," Mother said. "Do you believe in spirits or ghosts?"

"You know there are no such things as ghosts. I'll prove it to you. I will sleep in Sarah's room tonight and you let her sleep with you," Father responded.

Mother thought about it. How foolish she would feel if nothing happened when Father was in the room. But Father persisted and she agreed to the arrangement saying we'll tell Sarah that it was a sleepover and no boys were allowed.

Franky and his dad unloaded the car, while his mother carried a half-asleep Sarah up to hers and her husband's room. As she climbed the stairs she thought, "Sarah is so sleepy maybe I won't have to explain anything." She entered the room and laid her daughter on the bed. Sarah's eyes immediately popped wide open.

"Why are we in your room Mommy?" Sarah asked.

"Well, I thought it would be fun if we had a girl's only sleepover tonight."

"Yeah!" Sarah yelled.

"Would you like some Kool-aid and popcorn for our pajama party, Sarah?" Mother asked.

Sarah quickly said yes and ran down the hall into Franky's room and began teasing him about his not being allowed to come to the all girl pajama party.

Franky was to tired too argue so he stuck his tongue out at Sarah and told her he didn't care, he didn't want to come to the pajama party anyway. He had to get some rest because they were taking the canoe out tomorrow. As Franky dozed off to sleep he heard the eagle calling out to him.

Chapter 16

Downstairs in the kitchen Father kissed his wife, saying, "I'm bushed, I'm going to call it a night."

"Okay, honey, I'll come in and see my Mr. Tuff Guy after our 'girls only party,'" Mother chuckled. She finished popping the popcorn and filled two glasses with Kool-aid and then headed upstairs to her room where Sarah was waiting. They watched a little television, ate their popcorn and talked about the circus. Sarah began yawning a lot, they were both tired, and so they decided it was time to go to sleep. Sarah was asleep almost as soon as her head hit the pillow.

Mother quietly slipped out of the room and walked down the hall to Sarah's room to join her husband. Father was sitting on the edge of the bed looking over his business journal.

"How is my tuff guy doing?" Mother asked.

Father chuckled and said, "I'm having a little trouble with the girly stuff, and I don't know if I can sleep with all those dolls staring at me. How many dolls does Sarah have anyway, a hundred?"

"You're not trying to chicken out are you?" Mother asked.

"No way, I'm the tuff guy champ, remember?" Father responded, laughing.

Mother kissed her husband good night again, and went back to her room. As she walked down the hall she wondered if he would hear the baby cry. Then she fussed at herself for being so foolish and ridiculous and gently crawled into bed next to Sarah to go to sleep.

In Sarah's room where Father was sleeping, the quiet was broken by the sound of a baby crying. This woke Father, and upon hearing it he sat straight up.

Suddenly, he began to sweat as if he had been running a marathon. "This is crazy, there has got to be a logical explanation why I hear a baby crying," Father said out loud. "This is just a dream and I am hearing a baby because of the talk Mother and I had before going to sleep."

Father got up and went to the bathroom, then straight back to bed. He was almost asleep when he heard it again. This time it was loud and clear. This time there was no mistaking what he had heard.

"What's going here, why can't I wake up? This has got to be a dream," he thought.

His heart was racing, and he felt a sense of panic rising within him. He rolled over, and felt his eyes being drawn toward the door he had bolted shut when they first moved in. He felt weightless, like he was floating, and a gentle wind seemed to be pulling him toward the bolted door. Just when he thought he would smash into the door, it mysteriously opened, and he floated through it. After going through the doorway, he felt himself being lifted up to the top of the room. As he floated up, he looked to see if he was going to hit the ceiling, but he saw the sky instead.

It was a clear moonlit night, but he saw three flashes of lightning and heard an eagle call out. As he hovered at the top of the room, he saw something floating down. He watched the object until it landed in the far corner on what appeared to be an old bundled up blanket.

Father could not believe his eyes. The attic was lit up as if it was day. The sound of the baby crying had stopped after he floated into the attic. But, now the crying started again. He was sure it was coming from the corner where the blanket was.

"Where did that blanket come from, I know it wasn't there when I bolted the door shut," Father thought.

All at once he felt himself moving again. He seemed to be drifting toward the blanket. As he looked at it, he saw that it was red and yellow stripe, just as Mother had described it.

Father reached for the blanket and the baby's crying softened. As he grabbed the edge of the material, the crying stopped. The blanket felt old and it crumbled in his hand from being so dry-rotted. As Father blew the dust out of his hand he looked down and saw that it was an eagles's feather that had fallen from the sky.

Lying on the old blanket beside the eagle feather was Franky's medallion. "How did that get in here?" Father thought to himself.

The crying started up again and was really loud. Father reached out again to touch the blanket, and as he did the crying stopped. All of a sudden he became aware of the darkness that now surrounded him. Complete total darkness filled the attic. He couldn't ever remember being in such darkness. He was really scared now and could not make his legs work. Father began to feel as if he couldn't breathe, and he panicked even more. Now he was hearing bells ringing in his head from lack of oxygen. At the very point he thought his lungs would explode, he woke up in Sarah's bed. The ringing in his head turned out to be the telephone ringing in the next room.

As he sat up in Sarah's bed listening to his wife talking to someone on the phone, his mind was racing with a thousand and one questions; none of which he seemed to have answers to. He got up and went to the bathroom to wash his face. His hands would not stop shaking. He kept telling himself over and over, "It was only a dream, it was only a dream."

After returning to Sarah's room, he could see from the light coming in the window, that her bed was a mess, and wet with his perspiration. He picked up the blanket and shook it out, and as he did an eagle's feather fell out of the fold in the blanket.

As the feather floated to the floor, Father became numb and just stared at it. Although he wanted to tell his wife what had happened, he could not make himself move. So he sat there numbly trying to sort out what he had witnessed only a short time before.

Father heard a faint knocking at Sarah's door, but he couldn't move to answer. It was Franky.

"Sarah, have you..." Franky began as he opened the door. When he entered Sarah's room, he saw his father just sitting on the edge of her bed staring at the floor.

"Hey, what are you doing here? I was expecting to find Sarah. Dad, are you all right?" His father did not answer.

Franky became very scared and started yelling, "Mom! Mom! Come quick! Something's wrong with Dad!"

Franky's mom came running into the room and saw her husband just sitting there on the edge of Sarah's bed. He was soaking wet and very pale.

"What is it honey? What's wrong?" she asked him, but her husband could not speak. All he could do was point to Franky's medallion on the table beside the bed. "Franky," Mother said, "take your medallion and go to your room. I need to talk to Dad."

"There it is…I was wondering what happened to my medallion," Franky said as he walked over and picked it up. Turning to leave, he asked, "Mom, is Dad going to be all right?" Franky was scared. He had never seen his dad like this before.

"Yes, I'm sure he'll be just fine, please go to your room. We will talk later," Mother replied.

Franky left the door open hoping to be able to listen to their conversation, but his mother shut the door behind him. He stood quietly trying to hear what his parents were saying. Franky listened hard and heard his mother say, "What happened? Did you hear the baby crying too?"

The more questions she asked the more his father seemed able to talk. Finally, Franky heard his dad telling her about his dream. Father apologized over and over for not believing his wife when she had the dream. Franky's curiosity was really running wild now. "How could a dream make his dad so upset?" he thought.

Squatting down, Franky tried to get a look through the crack in the door, but all he saw was a pair of legs. Suddenly, the door opened and Franky looked up to see his mother looking down at him with one of those special looks only a mother can give.

"Are you looking for something?" Mother asked.

Franky was about to answer when Father called out, "Franky come here."

Franky, glad for the chance to not have to explain to his mom why he was eavesdropping, went nervously into the room. "Yes, Dad," he replied, still feeling uneasy.

"I am afraid that we will have to put off the canoe ride today," Father said, knowing that Franky would be disappointed.

"Why?" asked Franky, already knowing that something was wrong. "Is everything alright?"

Father began to explain about his dream and how it tied into Sarah and his mother's dreams. He had decided to go into town and talk to George. Since George and his family had owned the property prior to the Thomas Family, he thought maybe one of them would know something that would help get to the bottom of this.

"Can I go? I want to visit the old Indian. I have had some strange dreams myself, except I was outside for most of them, maybe they all fit together! Did you know, Dad, that the family of the old Indian was killed on this property?" Franky rambled. He was so excited he didn't wait for his father to answer and went on to tell him all that he had learned about the Indians. His dad was surprised to hear of all the trouble the old Indian had faced, and he was also very surprised that Franky had not mentioned it before now.

He told Franky he could go with him into town. Franky started to leave Sarah's room to go to his own to get dressed when he thought about the story about the medallion and asked his father if he remembered it.

"Yes, I remember," said his dad. "It is supposed to warn a person's spirit of danger and other things that are around. Why do you ask me that Franky?"

"Well, it just dawned on me that each time you guys had that dream the medallion was in here," answered Franky. "I think somehow, it may be connected."

"You know, you just might have a point," replied Father as he thought back of each time one of them had the dream.

Chapter 17

Franky's mother called up the stairs for them to come and eat breakfast. As they were eating, Franky's dad told Mother he was going into town to talk to George. She agreed that this was about the only thing left to try.

After breakfast, Franky went outside to wait. Father sat sipping his coffee as Mother cleaned up.

"Do you think that some spirit is trying to contact us?" Mother asked. In spite of Father's look of disbelief, Mother continued, "Think about it, our dreams, your dream, and how did that eagle feather get in the bed? Why did we only dream when we were in Sarah's room? The medallion never gave Franky any bad dreams when it was in his room."

"I don't know about all that spirit stuff," Father said, "but I'm going to see if George can tell us anything."

He walked over and kissed his wife goodbye, and told her not to hold lunch. He didn't know how long they would be.

Franky saw his father coming out of the house and ran ahead and got in the car. He was barely able to control his excitement. Franky loved a good mystery, and this one was a doosy.

As they were driving into town, Father was thinking back to the conversation he had with the waitress at the diner, that first night they were in town. He remembered her saying how the last family that had lived in the house left suddenly in the middle of the night. Father wondered if this same nightmare thing had happened to them. He had not thought much about that conversation until now, however, he was really beginning to wonder.

Father pulled into George's office parking lot and parked. He told Franky to stay in the car until he spoke with George. Father walked up to the receptionist in George's office, "Hello, is George in?"

"No, I'm sorry, he's not in yet, but I expect him about any time. Would you like to have a seat and wait?" the kind woman replied from behind the old desk.

"Yes, thank you," Father said, and walked over and sat down.

"Well, good morning!" George said as he came in the side door, "What can I do for you?"

"Well," Father began reluctantly, "It is a little confusing, but I would like to talk to you about the history of our house."

"Sure," replied George, "just as soon as I check in on the old Indian."

Father was surprised to know the Indian had been in the back room all that time. He never made a sound.

George came back in and asked, "So what brings you in here today, Mr. Thomas. I hope you're not having plumbing problems or anything?"

"No," Father said half laughing. "I wish it were that simple." Father slowly began telling George about all the dreams Sarah and his wife had been having. As he went on, he told George of the dream and how he had heard the baby crying and of the blanket, the eagle feather and about Franky finding a medallion.

Up to this point George had listened without commenting. He interrupted Father's speech and said, "Tell me about the medallion Franky found. What does it look like?"

As Father described the medallion, George began to smile. "Your boy found a dream catcher. You know, the other family who lived in your house before you had a son about Franky's age. I made him a dream catcher out of willow and sinew. That boy was a very adventuresome little guy; he loved exploring, and what an imagination he had!"

"He sounds a lot like Franky!" exclaimed Father.

"I guess I need to get to know Franky better," said George.

At this Father laughed and said, "I'm his father and I can't say that I really know him. Especially when his imagination gets started."

Chapter 18

George chuckled, thinking of his own experiences when he was young. Suddenly the door to George's office flew open and Franky came running in.

"Dad, you gott'a feel this medallion, something is happening to it. It's humming with energy or something, it's kinda like vibrating!" Franky said excitedly.

It was at that exact moment that the old Indian began to sing. He was singing in the language of his childhood. "He is singing his traveling song, as if he is leaving and not coming back," Franky said.

Father looking shocked asked Franky how he knew that. Franky could not really answer this.

He said calmly, "I don't know how I know, Dad, I just know."

It was then that George realized something strange was happening. He told Franky and his father that he would meet them at their house later that day. George was not sure exactly how or why, but somehow Franky's dream catcher humming and vibrating, the attic in their house and the old Indian singing were all connected.

This was the first time that George had ever heard the old Indian speak anything. George had been caring for the old Indian a very, very long time.

Father couldn't have agreed with George more. Something strange was happening indeed. In fact, this was so strange that Father was very glad that George was coming to their home later that day, just so another person would confirm that what was happening was real.

The drive home was very quiet. Franky, much to his father's surprise, was sound asleep in the car. This left Father to his own thoughts as he drove down the dusty roads, trying to understand the connection that George also seemed to see.

Unknown to Father, Franky's thoughts were far from the car on that old road. In his slumber he remembered feeling extremely tired and that he could not stay awake.

Franky opened his eyes and realized he was in the woods. As he walked, he began to smell smoke. He heard a voice crying in the distance with such agony and sorrow that it caused something deep within him to moan. He kept following the sound until he came upon the village, or what used to be the village. He looked around and now could see where the smoke was coming from.

The village was on fire, and the crying was from his uncle, "Walking Bear." He was desperately looking for his wife and baby. Franky tried to go to him but something was holding him back by his shoulders.

"Franky, Franky, we're home," Father said as he gently shook him by the shoulders.

He opened his eyes and was confused for a second about where he was. As he stumbled out of the car, Franky looked around, he distinctly heard the call of an eagle. Franky looked upward and searched the bright blue sky for the bird. While he was looking at the sky, suddenly he saw three flashes of lightning. "Man, that's weird," thought Franky.

"Franky, would you go get my tools from the little shed?" Father asked.

George pulled up just as Franky came out of the shed with the tools. When Franky walked up to where Father was, George had already gotten out of the car and was speaking with Father about the room they were getting ready to open. George, being more in tune with the spiritual side of the Indian ways, was explaining to Father how he thought that the spirits had used the dream catcher and Franky's own spiritual awareness to bring peace back to the old Indian. He said he also thought it was meant to help teach the rest of the family a little about spiritual things. Father was not sure about what he was hearing, but at this point he just wanted an answer, any answer.

"I have a strong sense that we are going to find the answer to all of this in your attic space," George said.

It wasn't until he heard a deep voice speaking in a native language that Franky noticed that George had brought the old Indian with him.

"As far as I am concerned, that is more proof of some connection," George said, as he pointed to the old Indian. "This is only the second time I have ever heard him talk. I have known him as far back as I can remember into my childhood. I just wonder what he is saying?"

Without any hesitation, Franky announced, "He's praying and thanking the spirits for bringing his child home."

George and Franky's father both looked at Franky at the same time and asked, "How do you know that?" Just like before in George's office, Franky could not explain how he knew, he just knew.

Father started getting a little nervous about entering the attic space. His memory of the horrible night terror he had experienced the night before was all too fresh.

Afraid he would lose his nerve, he said, "Come on, let's get this over with." He was thankful that his wife had taken Sarah for a walk to gather wild flowers.

George, Franky and Franky's father all went up to Sarah's room and opened the door to the attic. As they stepped in, the darkness closed around them. Father began feeling the same shortness of breath he felt in his dream, and began to panic.

George quickly turned on the flashlight that he had brought. "In your dream, where did you see the blanket, Mr. Thomas?"

Father pointed to the far right-hand corner of the room. As he stepped forward he felt a slight breeze as if something had brushed by him. When he turned to look, he saw it was the old Indian. He was moving in the direction Franky's father had pointed. He moved with the quickness of a nine-year-old boy instead of a man well over one-hundred years old.

As the old Indian reached the spot where Franky's dad had seen the blanket, they heard him let out a very loud moan. It was such a cry of anguish and sorrow that it brought tears to their own eyes. They were feeling the pain this old Indian brave had felt all these years as he searched for his child. His only desire was to reunite his missing son with his wife, "Laughing Eyes."

George pointed his flashlight in the direction of the old Indian. There on the floor were bits and pieces of a blanket, the same blanket Franky's mother and father had seen in their dream. Resting on the very edge of the blanket was an eagle feather.

Even though the blanket was almost non-existent due to decay, the blanket clearly held a tiny form. It was the skeletal remains of an infant child.

As they all stood there in disbelief of what they were seeing, they heard the old Indian speaking. Though they could not understand what the old Indian brave was saying, it was obvious to all that he was praying. They remained there, in silence, unable to speak, listening to the old Indian pray. There was no doubt in any of their minds that this prayer was a prayer of sorrow, happiness, as well as thankfulness and preparation.

When he had finished his prayer, he reached down carefully and picked up the remains of the blanket with his son's skeleton enclosed. He walked past George, Franky and Franky's dad, taking the bundle outside to the field behind the house.

It was then that Franky broke the silence and said, "WOW!!"

Chapter 19

George had been raised with and around Indians most of his life. So, he had a pretty good understanding of the Indian ways. He was beginning to see the whole picture and was trying to explain what was happening to Franky's father.

Franky's father was still kind of confused, even though he witnessed the whole story unfold right before his very eyes.

When George finished with his brief explanation Franky's dad said, "Well, I guess I just don't get it."

George could see that Mr. Thomas seemed to be completely dumbfounded. He was trying very hard to understand how the eighty-year-old bones of an Indian baby could appear in the attic of a house that had not even been built when the baby was murdered.

"How did the eagle feathers appear out of thin air, and how did that eagle fly through our attic?" asked Franky's dad. George laughed at Mr. Thomas' total confusion, and said, "Obviously this is going to take much more time than we have right this minute. How about after this is all over with, in a couple of days I will come back out and take some time to try to help you to understand everything?"

That sounded real good to Franky's dad, so they all turned and followed the old Indian out to the field behind the house. They watched as he was preparing the body of his child for burial.

As they all stood by silently watching, Franky's mom came home. As she crossed the lawn, she could see Franky, her husband and George standing in the field behind their house, so she joined them. Once she got a little closer she could then see the old Indian.

The look on her face was enough to tell her husband that she recognized the blanket as the same one that was in her dream and that she also knew what was wrapped up in it.

"Let's go in the house and let him finish in peace," George said. "I will explain what he is doing the best I know how." They all agreed and went into the house.

Mother made coffee for George, Father and also herself, then poured a glass of milk for Franky.

"Where's Sarah?" asked Franky's dad.

"Oh, I saw George's car in the drive, and wasn't sure what was going on so I took her over to the neighbor's house to play with Jenny," Mother explained.

"That was a good idea, hon, as you can see things might be a little scary for Sarah," Father added.

George attempted to explain to them what the Indian was doing, and why they were the ones the spirits chose to reunite the old Indian and his family. He told Mother and Father that they themselves must be of the same native line as the old Indian, and that was why they were more connected to the spirits. Franky certainly seemed to be directly connected to the old Indian in some way.

Father, who was listening while watching the Indian through the window, interrupted by asking George, "What's he doing now?"

George looked out the window and told him the Indian was using sage and sweet grass to bless the ground and to purify his son's body in preparation for burial. He also explained that the spirits of the Indian's son and wife could be at peace now, along with the soul of the old Indian, since they would all soon be reunited.

Franky was having a hard time being patient. He was absolutely fascinated with what the old Indian was doing and he wanted to be out there with him.

It seemed like hours to Franky before the Indian motioned for them to come out. Even though they didn't understand everything that was going on, they were at least willing to accept it and help in any way they could.

The Indian motioned them to sit down on the ground around him, and as they did he spoke to them in English. "I give you thanks for your help in reuniting my family."

Looking at Franky, he said "To you 'Little Cou...' stopping himself he quickly added, "'little one,' for always following your heart, even when others thought you were daydreaming or making mischief." Looking at Franky's parents, he said, "To you for being the parents who believed in your dreams and also the dreams of your children. Allowing them to follow their heart, as you have followed yours."

Then he turned to George and said, "I give thanks to you and your family for your kindness to me and the special care that you have given to the land that I was born on and will be returned to. I know you do not fully understand my people's ways, as our ways are different from those of the white man's, but I will try to answer your questions."

Father asked, "How is it possible for your son's remains to show up in our attic, when at the time your son died this house wasn't even built yet?"

"Never doubt the power of the spirits. When the spirits were convinced that I was true to the words that I had spoken so long ago, and was determined to live in peace, they brought your family here to help me reunite with my wife and child. The eagles brought my child to you. The Creator, or Kijjii Wasii Monato, guides us in many ways. Kijjii Wasii Monato is the name my people call the one that created all things. It is through his creation that we all are connected to each other and to the Creator. He is the life of all things—the trees, the birds, the four-legged ones and the two-legged ones. All things that walk or crawl on our sacred mother, Gia Tula, Turtle Island are all connected. What we do to the Earth, to each other or anything on the earth, we do to ourselves and to the Creator. Our thoughts and words leave us and manifest in the spirit world and then return to us and manifest here in the material world. That is why we must truly do that which is right at all times, for what you do and speak returns to you."

Franky was overwhelmed with excitement. "That's the same thing that the great bear and the one who said he was my uncle told me."

Father interrupted Franky with, "WHAT BEAR?! And just who is this man who claims he's your uncle?"

The old Indian interrupted to explain how that Franky had been receiving teachings from the spirits in his dreams and journeys that he sometimes took. He went on telling them, "This is how all that you see now has come about. In due time all things will be understood. This is the way of the spirits, to teach through dreams and children and in their time not ours."

"Now I must ask one more thing of you. My son must be buried near his mother and on this land to finish his journey. It is a tradition to allow the spirit of his mother to find him. My son's spirit was very strong; he did not go to sleep in the spirit world and leave me to die in my grief. Now I must in turn honor him by completing the rest of his journey, as well as my own. I must go to get some things so that I can prepare for my journey. I grow weary and my time is not long. Would you sit with my son until I return? It is our custom to not leave the bodies of those who have crossed over to the spirits alone until they are reunited with the Mother, Gia Tula."

Mother quickly answered, "Yes, it would be an honor," to which Father agreed.

Franky was suddenly very sad because he understood the old Indian was preparing for his own death. Franky knew he would miss him terribly.

Chapter 20

George, who had been silent up to now, stood up and asked the old Indian if he was ready to go back to town to get his things. The old Indian replied yes.

After George and the Indian left, Father and Mother began talking about all the strange things that had happened in the last few days while Franky sat close by daydreaming.

Father said that if Sarah had never taken Franky's medallion none of this might have come about.

"Oh! Sarah!" exclaimed Mother, "I better go get her."

"Maybe you should wait; we are still not sure what is going to happen."

Mother agreed, and went inside to call the neighbors to see if Sarah could stay a while longer.

While she was gone, Franky's father watched Franky and wondered what he was thinking about. He appeared to be in another trance or something. Father knew that he would not take Franky's daydreaming as a lack of responsibility or a childish past time ever again.

Franky's imagination had taken him back to the creek. He was standing next to the creek and the great bear had come to talk to him.

"Walking Bear is preparing for his journey into the spirit world. You must help him prepare," said the great bear.

"What do I have to do?" asked Franky.

"Listen carefully and learn," said the great bear. "There is much to be done."

The great bear taught Franky how to build a sweat fire, about each stone to be used, and how to remove the stones from the fire and take them to the Indian. To Franky it seemed as though the great bear talked to him for hours instructing him on what to do to help with the ceremony that was about to begin.

"Little Cougar, the time has come. I must go so you may begin the preparations." With this, the great bear turned to leave.

Franky asked, "When will you come back?"

"As you need me, I will be there."

"But what if I forget all this? I don't want to make a mistake," Franky said.

"Trust yourself, trust the spirits that guide you, they will help you make good decisions."

The great bear turned and walked off into the woods. When Franky opened his eyes, he saw his mom coming from the house with George and the Indian.

"Sarah is going to spend the night at the neighbors, oh, and I put on another pot of coffee." With that she returned to the house to finish some chores.

As the old Indian approached, he asked Franky, "Will you help me with the preparations and the cleansing ceremony?"

Franky replied, "Yes."

The old Indian gave Franky a bundle of something wrapped in a bear's hide.

"This is my medicine bundle; I will not need it any longer. I'm giving it to you. In the days and years to come you will be visited by the spirits to teach you how to use it."

Father and George both told the old Indian that they would help in any way they could.

"Thank you," said the Indian. "Would one of you gather some water from the creek while the other watches over my son? Franky, I need you to search for wood to build a fire. I am going to search for the right stones for my purification sweat."

They each went their separate ways to accomplish the things the Indian had asked of them, with George staying behind to watch the infant's remains. The search for the proper stones took a little while and it soon became too dark to see.

"Could someone build a small fire off to the side to help light the night and to take the chill out of our bodies?" the Indian asked.

George and Father built the fire and Mother joined them with a thermos of hot coffee, sandwiches and blankets for everyone. Soon they were all sitting around the fire relaxing, listening to the popping and crackling as the flames consumed the wood.

Except for the sound of the fire, there was complete silence, each of them absorbed in their own thoughts. Mother went back to the house to pray and rest while the men stayed at the fire and watched over the old Indian and his son.

Chapter 21

As the night passed, it seemed they all had visions and dreams of the way things were and what was to happen in the morning. Franky seemed to be the one most visited.

At several times during the night he had many dreams. In his dreams, he witnessed many different spirits coming to speak with the old Indian. As one dream would end, another would begin. Franky saw the old Indian speak with the Bear, a Wolf, Eagle, and Panther. There were other Indians there too. Franky heard a drum and watched as they all danced in preparation of the coming ceremony.

In the morning, Franky was the first one to wake. He saw the Indian, who had spent the night in prayer and meditation, standing facing the sun with a pipe holding it up as an offering and singing the most beautiful song that Franky had ever heard. This was a memory that Franky would recall many times through the remaining years of his life.

When the Indian had finished the song, he told Franky it was time to begin. He turned to Franky's father and George, and asked if they would gather some of the young willow trees from around the creek. He described the size and the amount needed, also the proper way to remove the trees. Franky's father and George quickly departed for the creek. They completed this task rather quickly.

While they were gone, Franky, under the watchful eye of his Indian friend began building the sweat fire. It wasn't long before the willow trees had been gathered and the fire wood put properly in place around the stones, which had been carefully chosen by the Indian the night before.

With the assistance of the old Indian, George and Franky's dad built a lodge. The completion of the last task was finally finished and their timing was perfect. As George was placing the last tree branch on the lodge, Franky's mother called them to come in for breakfast. Franky was afraid to leave the old Indian, but his Indian friend assured him it would be okay. The only task left to be done was the covering of the lodge. This was to be done with deer hides that were in George's car. George and the Indian went to the car to retrieve the hides.

"Go now, nourish your bodies, my friends. The remainder of the tasks to be done I must do alone," said the old Indian.

Franky really didn't want to go into the house to eat. His father, however, insisted, so Franky reluctantly followed along. He was too nervous and excited to eat so he stood watching the Indian dancing around the area where the sweat fire was to be.

As he watched, there was a call of an eagles and then a loud clap of thunder as lightning flashed and struck the ground around the Indian. Franky closed his eyes to the bright light.

When he reopened his eyes, the fire was again burning with fierce flames. "Wow, the lightning hit the wood and caught it on fire!" he exclaimed. Everyone came over to the window to watch.

Franky watched impatiently from the window, just waiting for a sign from the Indian for them to come out. When at last the Indian made the sign, Franky bolted out the door.

"My friends, the time has now come for us to prepare the two burial spots," remarked the old Indian.

He then handed Franky's father an acorn. He instructed him to plant the acorn above him on his burial spot, so the circle of life could be completed. Seeing the puzzled look on Father's face, the old Indian explained. "Warriors kill the deer for food to feed their families. When we go to the Great Spirit, our body returns to our Mother Earth. An acorn is planted with us. Our bodies nourish it into a great oak tree. In turn, the oak tree provides food for the deer's children; thus completing the circle of life."

Father was a little confused and surprised by the explanation given by the Indian about the completion of the circle of life.

George walked up to the Indian and asked him where they should begin the digging. He was not surprised by the old Indians reply.

"Listen to the spirits, my friend, just listen to the spirits."

The Indian asked Franky to walk with him while the others finished digging the graves.

Franky and his friend walked toward the field and woods. As they walked, the Indian began showing Franky areas that were sacred to his people and asked him to care for the land and to always walk close to the spirits. He began to tell him of a man who came to the Shawanwa people (Shawnee), who they called Chezus. He continued to speak to Franky, saying…

This man was said to have come from the clouds. He taught that we had forgotten the old ways, that as a people we did not walk in balance with our brothers and sisters of the animal world or Nature, or with each other as a people. And by not walking in balance with this world, we did not walk in balance with our spiritual world, or our Creator.

This man taught us of ways to be reconnected with our Creator. It was said that if we did these things as we were shown, we would remain connected to the Creator. To this day it is so.

It had also been taught that we had everything, we had no worries and we took advantage of this and began to neglect our Creator and our spiritual side of life. So to remind us of our human nature, the Creator sent a plant that was beautiful to behold and seemed to be plentiful. This plant turned to a demon. It caused the people to turn red in blotches that seeped liquid and itched terribly. This demon plant spread its venom all over the people, and finally our medicine people were shown that it was because the people had forgotten the ways of the Creator. There was much fasting, praying and ceremony until the Creator heard us and allowed the medicine people to know the herb to use to relieve the itch of this curse. The plant is known as Poison Ivy today and the herb that is given to help is called Jewel Weed.

It was also taught that we came from the Creator and we will return to the Creator, as our bodies will return to our mother,

GiaTula, the earth. To represent this, our ceremony areas were set up in a circle and there was a pole of cedar planted in the middle. There was a cross piece of cedar wood that was put on this pole. The pole planted in the ground was a connection of energy between the Earth Mother and our Creator. The cross piece was a reminder to us that we walk in balance with the Creator, the Earth and her children as well as each other.

There is today what is known as the medicine wheel, this is a symbol of the ceremony grounds of most tribes. This is my understanding of the medicine wheel. It is a circle with a cross in it, like the ceremony circle. Each point is a direction as well as a door to that direction. A color, a plant, an animal or spirit-helper guide represent each direction. The center is where the Creator resides (the Creator comes out of the East direction.) All things revolve around the center. There are twelve main ceremonies that are performed as we walk the medicine wheel of life each year as a tribe. They are each done in accordance to the directions and seasons. There are four main directions; they are east, south, west, and north. Each has its own guardian, herb and animal.

EAST—WABIN MANATO is the spirit of this direction, the spirit animal is the Eagle. This direction represents new beginnings, new life, and new understandings. This is time of spring, the seeds are planted for the crops or food. (Spiritually as well.)

SOUTH—SAWAN MANATO (Sha-wen) is the spirit of this direction, the spirit animal is the Red tail hawk (mysquelenyi) and the deer (pesegthi). This is the time of new growth, the seeds planted in the east are growing taking root. (Spiritually and physically)

WEST—KILISQAU MANATO is the spirit of this direction. This is the direction where we come from and walk to. This spirit is the keeper of the spirits, this is also where we examine ourselves inwardly to see if our growth is good, (spiritually) and this is also the place of the black bear or medicine bear. We pray for our physical healing of this direction.

NORTH—KIWIDEN MANATO is the spirit of this direction. This is the place of the white bear. This is the direction of knowledge, both spiritually and physically. This is a direction where we learn our crafts and gain knowledge of what we have experienced in the other directions. This is a place of hard times, of winter and survival.

We each walk our own path in each of these directions but we also walk it together as a people. In your time it is hard to find one who cares about another. The people are all too busy to worry about our mother, Gia Tula, (the earth/ environment) or each other. Your main work is to learn the old ways, listen to the guides that the Creator sends you and teach the people to help each other and remember the Creator and the creation. You must teach all who will hear how to walk in balance and harmony with Nature, each other, and the Creator.

Little Cougar, you are of the seventh generation. It is the prophecy that the spirit of Tecum8a will return to unite the people and once again the people will walk in balance with each other, the Creator and their mother earth, GiaTula. Listen to your heart, trust in yourself, and walk in balance. Wasikatwelokiwisilawaype audein uhuk

(Let us always do good and be blessed)

Although he didn't understand everything, Franky would remember the words of the old Indian for the rest of his life. Meanwhile, George and Father were trying to dig in the ground.

Chapter 22

Father said, "This is like digging in concrete." George agreed.

Pausing a moment he looked around. Franky's Father suddenly noticed a difference in the color of the ground.

"I wonder why this is so different, I never noticed this before." Father walked over and stuck the shovel into the dirt and it went in like it was going into sand. "I think this is where the spirits want the graves to be." George agreed, and they began digging in the softened dirt.

The digging was now effortless; they didn't even break a sweat even though the sweat fire close to them was burning so high.

"George, do you notice anything weird about this fire?" Father asked. Not giving George a chance to answer, he continued, "This is the coldest fire that I have ever been around."

"You know, you're right, how strange," responded George.

"George, what did our Indian friend mean when he told me to plant an acorn above him on *his* burial spot?"

"He has found his peace. When this is over, we will be singing the travel song for him," responded George sadly.

"I was afraid of that," said Father. "Now I understand why we are digging two graves."

Father was feeling extremely sad because he now understood that they were helping the old Indian prepare for his own death. Although Father did not know the old Indian brave very well, he respected him greatly and knew, as well as all who had come in contact with him, that he would miss him.

Mother came out of the house with a pitcher of lemonade and some glasses. "Where did the Indian and Franky go?" she asked. "They've been gone a while. I'm starting to get a little worried."

"I wouldn't worry about them. The spirits are protecting them, and we have learned that the spirits are certainly real," answered Father. "Look there they are now."

The Indian spoke to George and Father, telling them that it was time to return his son, "Little Star," to his mother. As the Indian carefully placed cedar, tobacco, sage and sweet grass in the hole, the others could hear him praying. "Kijjii Wasii Manito Peoau Ah Dein U Huk, Wabin Manito Peoau Ah Dein U Huk, Kilausqau Manito Peoau Ah Dein U Huk, Kiwi Den Manito, Peoau Ah Dein U Huk."

After he was finished, the Indian lovingly placed the body of his son into the bosom of the sacred Mother Earth, Gia Tula.

An eagle began to circle the area above the grave and called four times, and as it flew away toward the west, something gently floated down to the ground, gently gliding on the breeze until it was so close they could all see it was a single feather.

The feather landed directly on Little Star. As soon as the feather touched the bones of the infant there were again three flashes of lightning.

At that moment tears filled every eye and deep inside they all knew that the spirits had received Little Star home.

The Indian breathed a deep sigh, it felt like it was a sigh of relief, and then he turned, grabbed a shovel and began to fill in the hole until the remains of his son was covered. He asked the others if they would finish filling his son's grave while he prepared himself for his own journey.

Father and George filled the hole the rest of the way. As they shoveled the dirt into the grave, Franky could see a few tears trickling down their cheeks. He understood why. They were shedding tears for the pain and suffering the old Indian had endured because he had been alone, unable to find his son.

"My friends, do not shed any more tears for me," the Indian said, "for I am going home soon, but cry for those who are still walking in the dark and do not know the way of the spirits or the Creator." He looked at Father. "You have all been chosen to carry the message of the old ways to the people who seek them. Franky has been chosen as the messenger and a medicine man to heal the people's bodies and their souls. He will teach and lead many people."

As the Indian spoke, the Thomas family felt blessed that they had experienced all that had happened.

The Indian spoke to George and Father. "Now, it is time for me to go into the womb of my mother, will you watch until I am done?"

They agreed quickly, honored that he had asked them. "Franky, will you carry the stones to me?"

Franky shook his head yes, not trusting himself to be able to speak without crying. He remembered what the Great Bear had taught him, "Trust in yourself, trust the spirits to guide you."

The Indian went into the sweat lodge and Franky carried the stones to him, just like the spirits had shown him. When he was finished he closed the door and they waited.

The wait seemed so long. They heard the Indian singing and praying. They listened to the sound of the drum, and felt the presence of the spirits. Franky did not know if his parents and George could see the warriors dancing around the fire in time with the drum beats, but he saw them, each and every one of them.

The eagle returned and was circling overhead calling.

Suddenly, all was silent. The eagle gave one last call and flew away.

For what seemed like an eternity, not one sound could be heard anywhere. Everything was still, the wind, the birds, even the crickets and frogs in the woods. It all seemed like a dream.

The silence was broken by another call of an eagle coming from the west. As they all looked up to see the eagle, much to their surprise another eagle came from the east, south and north. Each of these four eagles, circling overhead, called to announce their arrival.

As Franky, his parents and George stood watching these four eagles circling and calling out, they could not help but notice there were no other sounds.

All at once, a loud clap of thunder roared and the lightning flashed once again. This time the lightning struck the ground four times all around them. The sky seemed to tear in half as if it had separated two worlds. The earth began to shake and rumble.

Franky's focus was glued to the sweat lodge. He could barely believe his eyes when he saw the warriors of the Indian's village appear and lift the old Indian up, gently placing him in the ground.

Franky rubbed his eyes and looked again. He once again saw the old Indian, except now he wasn't old anymore. As a matter of fact, he was the Indian from his visions. He was "Walking Bear."

Just as suddenly that all noise had stopped, it all began again. The birds were chirping, the breeze blew the trees, and the frogs and crickets sang their earthy songs. But, somehow everything was different.

Franky noticed that the sweat fire and lodge were gone, the warriors, and even Walking Bear had all disappeared. All that remained of the dream was a small medicine bundle, the Indian's pipe and a beautiful knife with a deer antler handle.

Where were Walking Bear and the sweat lodge? What happened to the fire? Where did everything go?

As Franky sat wondering what happened, he heard the voice of Walking Bear.

"Take the pipe and place it, the medicine bundle and the knife in the knot hole in the large oak tree. Your work has just begun Little Cougar. You must always listen to the spirits and trust yourself."

Franky began to cry, sad at the thought of not seeing his Indian friend again.

One more time Franky heard the voice of Walking Bear say, "Listen to your heart, Little Cougar, listen to your heart."

All at once Franky felt a weight on him and heard his sister Sarah excitedly yelling, "Wake up Franky! Wake up—it's moving day! Come on, wake up!"

After a long day of moving Franky was finally able to explore his new home. It was just like in his dream, the stained glass windows, winding staircase and even the kerosene lamps in his room.

Outside was the same too. As he approached the spot where the tree was in his dream, Franky stood stunned.

There in the tree was Walking Bear's pipe, medicine bundle and knife, exactly where Franky had put them.

Dreams are just dreams...or are they? Kijii monato au dein u huk peh (May the Great spirit bless you)

Printed in the United States
51525LVS00002B/4-21

9 781424 130481